The
Great Gathering

STANDING IN HOLY PLACES
BOOK ONE

THE GREAT GATHERING

BY CHAD DAYBELL

spring creek
BOOK COMPANY
Provo, Utah

ISBN 13: 978-1-932898-79-8
e. 1

Published by:
Spring Creek Book Company
P.O. Box 50355
Provo, Utah 84605-0355

www.springcreekbooks.com

Cover design © Spring Creek Book Company
Cover photo © Photographer: Rayna Canedy | Agency: Dreamstime.com

Printed in the United States of America
10 9 8 7 6 5 4 3 2 1
Printed on acid-free paper

Library of Congress Cataloging-in-Publication Data

Daybell, Chad, 1968-
  The great gathering / by Chad Daybell.
      p. cm. -- (Standing in holy places ; bk. 1)
  ISBN 978-1-932898-79-8 (pbk. : alk. paper)
  1. Families--Fiction. 2. Second Advent--Fiction. I. Title.

PS3554.A972G74 2007
813'.54--dc22
                                        2007023696

ACKNOWLEDGMENTS

I want to thank my wife, Tammy, who is always the first person to read my books. Her suggestions have greatly improved each book. I also appreciate her love and patience as the books are being written. I also appreciate the assistance my children have given in reading the manuscript and sharing helpful ideas.

I would like to thank my father, Jack Daybell. As my novels are taking shape, he makes key editing suggestions and catches crucial plot holes. His enthusiasm for my books has been a wonderful thing in my life.

Craig Huff and Jarom Huff also deserve mention for their encouragement in many ways throughout the years, and for their assistance with portions of this novel.

I also greatly appreciate Dianna Smith of Eden Bookshop in Independence, Missouri. She has enthusiastically promoted my previous novels and has patiently waited for this new series.

I do want to mention the following two books that were helpful in structuring the plot and selecting the locations of the story:

* *Prophecies: Signs of the Times, Second Coming, Millennium*
    by Matthew B. Brown
* *Sacred Sites: Searching for Book of Mormon Lands*
    by Joseph L. Allen

And most of all, thank you to everyone who read my previous novels and then asked for more to be written. I hope this new series meets your expectations.

AUTHOR'S NOTE

———— ✿ ————

I want to emphasize that this series is a work of fiction. While the events portrayed in the book are based on scriptural prophecies and the words of the prophets, the specific locations mentioned in the book were selected based on my knowledge and familiarity with these areas, rather than a prophecy or account that targets these particular cities.

The situations in the book are simply meant to serve as representations of what could happen anywhere in the world when the Saints are called to gather together by the leaders of the LDS Church.

The events of this series are set several years in the future, but my intent isn't to give a sense of security that these major occurrences are still a long way off. These events could easily happen sooner than are portrayed in these novels, and we must prepare ourselves for possible challenges. I want to emphasize, however, that this series is about developing faith and trust in the Lord, rather than acting in fear or haste.

I greatly appreciated the words of Elder Jeffrey R. Holland of the Quorum of the Twelve Apostles in the July 2007 issue of the *Ensign* magazine. In an article entitled "This, the Greatest of All Dispensations" he wrote, "As far as the timing of the triumphant, publicly witnessed Second Coming and its earthshaking events, I do not know when that will happen. *No one* knows. The Savior said that even the angels in heaven would not know (see Matthew 24:36)."

Elder Holland then continues, "We should watch for the signs, we should live as faithfully as we possibly can, and we should share the gospel with everyone so that blessings and protection will be available to all. But we must not be paralyzed just because that event and the events surrounding it are ahead of us somewhere. We cannot stop living life. Indeed, we should live life more fully than we have ever lived it."

I am grateful for Elder Holland's counsel on how we should prepare for the future, and I highly recommend you read the entire article, which is available at www.lds.org.

The First Presidency and the Quorum of the Twelve Apostles will always be there to guide us. Don't be misled by people who might "cry wolf." If we follow the words of the President of the Church, who is the Lord's living prophet, we will be prepared for whatever lies ahead.

For example, the First Presidency recently released a set of preparedness pamphlets under the title of *All Is Safely Gathered In*. These pamphlets are intended to motivate and guide the Saints to become better prepared for upcoming world events. Keep in mind that no matter what may come, if you are on the Lord's side of the battle, that is the right place to be.

Chad Daybell
July 2007

THE BEGINNING

This series begins more than a decade after the terrorist attacks of September 11, 2001 that killed thousands of people in New York, Pennsylvania, and Washington, D.C.

From that day, peace was taken from the earth until the Savior's Second Coming. The efforts to stop terrorism led to prolonged conflicts in Afghanistan, Iraq, and other countries. These events coincided with a steady string of natural disasters such as the tsunami that struck Indonesia in 2004, the flooding of New Orleans by Hurricane Katrina in 2005, and other troubles that followed throughout that decade.

The difficulties seemed to grow as U.S. President George W. Bush's term ended, and his successor faced several challenges on both national and international levels.

Steady inflation eroded the value of the dollar, and the trade deficit with countries such as China put the United States in a vulnerable economic position. The ongoing military clashes around the world stretched the limits of the U.S. armed forces, while the cost of living steadily climbed ahead of the average wage. As prices soared, homeless people were becoming a common sight across the United States.

Despite these troubles, Latter-day Saints had many reasons to remain optimistic, even after the death of the Church's beloved prophet, President Gordon B. Hinckley. His passing had long been expected, but it still came as a shock. A majority of Church members could not remember any other prophet. However, when the tributes to President Hinckley poured in from the world's leaders, the

Saints were able to reflect on what had been accomplished during his lengthy administration.

Under the inspired leadership of President Hinckley's successor, Thomas S. Monson, the Church continued to expand around the world at a rapid rate. Millions of new members joined the Church throughout Central and South America, and there were numerous conversions in European countries and parts of the United States that previously had been known as "difficult" missions.

The building of small temples around the world continued, and the Church began to be recognized as a powerful force for good in virtually every country. Whenever there was a major disaster, the Saints in the affected area would lead the way in organizing shelters and providing relief. Although the disasters were horrendous, these tragedies sparked interest among good Christian people about "those Mormons who are always helping out." The Church's membership totals continued to impressively escalate.

As the new century moved into its second decade, the battle between good and evil become more pronounced. In many ways the righteous became more devoted to the Lord, while the wicked became more brazen in their actions. Pornography was openly distributed in most of America's major cities, and many laws concerning moral issues were relaxed by the federal courts, thereby legalizing types of wickedness that previous generations never would have tolerated.

Sadly, many faithful Saints allowed themselves to be led astray by these many temptations, and the General Authorities were constantly warning that "even the very elect could be deceived." The problem of apostasy seemed even more pronounced in Utah, the Church's "home base." Large numbers of Saints became lax in their Sunday meeting attendance and other basic Church principles, creating deep personal and family problems.

Also, many families had tied themselves down to unnecessarily large homes with equally large mortgages, and bankruptcies were commonplace as the economy stalled. Crime was on the rise, and Salt Lake City turned into what President Heber C. Kimball had once prophesied it would become—"one of the wicked cities of the world."

With these mounting problems, some Saints speculated that the Savior's Second Coming couldn't be far off. However, others argued that many important prophecies still had to be fulfilled, such as the building of New Jerusalem and the return of the Lost Ten Tribes.

These kinds of debates caused additional members to leave the Church, saying that the prophecies and revelations of Joseph Smith and other prophets were outdated and impossible to fulfill. These former Church members openly challenged the General Authorities on nearly every issue through organized protests and press conferences that the media always covered extensively.

These were stressful times for righteous Saints, but they knew that the prophets' words were still in effect. The Lord was merely sifting and refining his flock for the great events that awaited them. The doubters and troublemakers wouldn't have to wait much longer for the prophecies to unfold.

Living amid this cultural commotion are three couples, all in their late 30s. They are loosely related and they have all known each other since their college years. They are active in their respective LDS wards and are making the most of their job opportunities and their family circumstances.

Here are their situations as this series begins:

Tad and Emma North

The Norths live with their three children in an apartment in Sandy, Utah. Their oldest son David just turned 16, while Charles is 11, and Leah is 8.

Tad is employed with a large accounting firm, and he commutes on the TRAX light-rail train each day to his office in the recently completed City Creek Center in Salt Lake City. His office is directly south of Temple Square, where the Crossroads Mall once stood.

Emma manages the family household and occasionally has worked from home as a freelance editor for a small LDS publishing company. She wrote a couple of books when she was younger and is getting the itch to write again.

Emma is saving her earnings for a down-payment on a house. The Norths had nearly bought a home when they were expecting Charles, but then he had been born seven weeks early. The doctors were amazed he had even survived, but thanks to good medical care and priesthood blessings, he is now a healthy, active child.

However, the hospital bills had nearly bankrupted them, and so after several years of tight finances, they are finally getting on their feet again. The TRAX line was just extended down through Utah County, and Tad could easily commute that far. Emma is now hoping they can soon buy a home in Springville, near her brother Doug's family.

Tad is serving as an Elders Quorum instructor, and Emma teaches Leah's Primary class.

Doug and Becky Dalton

The Daltons live in Springville with their two children. Justin is three, and Heather is one. They live in the same ward as Doug's parents, and they have a big backyard and a variety of pets.

Doug is Emma North's younger brother, and they have stayed close throughout the years. Becky and Emma have become good friends.

Doug and Becky had an on-and-off relationship during their college years. They met soon after Doug's mission to New Jersey, but then Becky felt she should serve a mission herself. After she returned home from the Canary Islands, they finally decided to get married.

Following their marriage in the San Diego Temple, they both only had one semester left at BYU to complete their bachelor's degrees. Once they graduated, they moved to Houston, Texas, where Doug completed an advanced degree in physical therapy, and Becky taught elementary school.

Three years later they returned to Utah and bought a home in south Springville. Doug found a good job with an Orem physical therapy company, and Becky was hired to teach fifth grade at Springville's Sage Creek Elementary, where she quickly became one of the most popular teachers.

Two years later, Becky became pregnant with their first child. She taught one more year of school and is now a stay-at-home mom. She admits Justin has a bit of a rebellious streak, and she is eager to send him to school as soon as possible!

Doug serves as his ward's Scoutmaster, and he takes the boys on week-long hikes in the Uinta Mountains each summer, camping on the site where his grandfather Keith Dalton operated a lumber mill in the late 1940s. Doug also considers himself somewhat of a World War II scholar, seemingly knowing more than most historians.

Becky is currently the ward nursery leader, partly because Heather was quite a handful for the previous leader. Surprisingly, Becky really enjoys the calling!

Josh and Kim Brown

The Browns had lived in Kansas ever since their marriage soon after Josh's mission. Josh graduated from Kansas State University and then with a law degree from nearby Washburn University. He opened a successful law practice in Omaha, Nebraska, where Kim's parents lived, and they were given plenty of opportunities to serve in the Church. Josh was called to be a bishop at age 32, and was then called to serve as the second counselor in the stake presidency.

Each spring they had visited the nearby Church historical sites in Missouri, such as the valley of Adam-ondi-Ahman, Liberty Jail, and the site in the city of Independence where the future New Jerusalem Temple would be built.

However, Kim's parents were recently called on a mission to serve in the Lima Peru Temple, so Josh and Kim took the opportunity to move closer to Josh's sister, Becky Dalton. Everything came together quickly. Josh accepted a position with a Provo law firm, and they found a house they liked in Spanish Fork.

Their one regret is that so far they have been unable to have a child. After years of miscarriages and seeing medical specialists, they still hold out hope for the blessing of having children.

Kim is a beautiful combination of her American father and Peruvian mother. She and her parents are converts to the Church. In fact, Josh is the missionary who baptized Kim, but they assure everyone they didn't start dating until after Josh's mission ended.

The year before Kim's family met the missionaries, her younger sister Tina had been killed in an auto-pedestrian accident. After Kim was baptized, she felt that Tina had accepted the gospel in the Spirit World and was eager to teach the gospel to their ancestors.

So Kim had completed Tina's temple ordinances, and for the past several years Kim had worked with her mother in compiling their family history. They had even traveled to Peru and met her mother's parents and grandparents, who had since joined the Church there and were serving in leadership positions.

Their family members in Peru had then worked together to accumulate thousands of family names, some of which reached back to the 1500s. In the process, both Josh and Kim had learned Spanish, and they both felt that learning the language might have a purpose beyond just family history work.

Having her parents now serving a mission in Peru had created a longing within Kim to also serve among the Spanish-speaking people, and she was praying for that chance.

Kim now works as a volunteer three days a week at the BYU Family History Center in the Harold B. Lee Library, where she is helping other people find their relatives. She also likes to spoil her nephew Justin and niece Heather by taking them for pizza at Chuck E. Cheese's in Orem every couple of weeks to give Becky a break from the kids.

As for Josh, after his various high-pressure callings in Nebraska, he is very content to serve as the secretary of his ward's High Priest group and hopes to stay in that calling for several years.

✤ ✤ ✤

Outside observers would consider these three couples to be typical, average Latter-day Saints in nearly every way. However, the Savior has always been aware of their spiritual strengths, and he has guided their decisions throughout their lives.

As His Second Coming draws near, the Lord will rely on them to help build His kingdom. As these six individuals trust in Him, they will soon accomplish monumental tasks they could barely have imagined.

This is their story. Who knows? Maybe this is your story, too.

CHAPTER 1

Emma North was stacking the last of the dishes in the kitchen cupboard when a deep rumble filled the apartment and the floor rippled. Framed photos fell from the walls, and Emma was knocked to her knees. The rumbling seemed to go on forever, and the computer screen clicked off as the power went out.

"Mom! Help!" The cry came from the kitchen where Emma's eight-year-old daughter Leah had been at the kitchen table eating lunch. Emma crawled back into the kitchen and found Leah crouched under the table with Spaghettios splattered all over her face and on the floor. Somehow she had kept the food out of her short blonde hair.

Emma huddled with Leah under the table until they were sure the earthquake was over. Then Emma glanced more closely at her daughter's messy face. "Oh, honey, let me help you," Emma said. She quickly cleaned Leah's face and wiped up the spilled food from the floor.

"My bowl was bouncing in front of me," Leah said. "Did I do good to get under the table?"

"Yes, you did," Emma replied as she took her daughter by the hand and walked to the front door of their simple three-bedroom apartment. They stepped onto the porch and saw mass confusion. Emma had planned for this last Saturday in October to include raking up an elderly neighbor's leaves and visiting a pumpkin patch with the kids, but it had turned into chaos.

Emma and Leah grabbed their jackets and began a slow, cautious walk to the church. Cars were pulled over to the side of the road, and most of Emma's neighbors were out on their lawns. Several large trees were toppled, and there were electrical wires sparking along the ground. The apartment building across the street had a crack right down the middle.

"I hope your brothers are okay," Emma said. Her sons David and Charles had gone to their ward building for a basketball practice with the Young Men. Suddenly her cell phone rang, which surprised her since the power was out. She answered and heard the worried voice of her husband Tad, who was putting in some overtime hours at his job in downtown Salt Lake City.

"Is everything all right?" Tad asked. "This quake seemed a lot stronger than the other ones we've been having."

"There is definitely a lot of damage in the neighborhood, but our apartment seems fine," Emma said. "I'm worried about the boys, though. I think I'll go get them."

"Probably stay home for now," Tad said. "They are just as safe at the church as they would be out on the streets. I am going to try to get home. I'll call you soon. I love you."

"I love you, too," Emma said before hanging up. A feeling of despair passed over her. This wasn't quite the life she had envisioned when she and Tad had married. After nearly two decades of "wedded bliss" they were still living in an apartment. The nation's economy was still chugging along, but it seemed that the cost of living always stayed ahead of Tad's wages.

Emma's thoughts were interrupted by the ringing of her cell phone. It was David, calling on the coach's cell phone from the church. "They're canceling practice," he said. "The basketball floor split apart."

"Well, that's a good reason," Emma said. "Is Charles okay?"

"He's fine, but a little scared," David said. "Brother Chappell wants our parents to come pick us up, though, rather than let us walk home alone."

"I'll be right there," Emma said.

She and Leah made their way down the sidewalk to the church. There were more than a few obstacles, such as a city electrical crew that had just pulled up to work on a fallen line, and a man standing with his hands on his hips as he surveyed the tree across his driveway. As they reached the church, they were surprised to see a corner of the building had collapsed, leaving a two-foot opening and a pile of bricks.

"Mom, over here!"

Emma saw her sons David and Charles standing on the lawn. "Does this mean we get to skip church tomorrow?" Charles asked with a grin.

"Maybe so," Emma said. "This looks worse than I thought it would."

Just then Brother Chappell came out of the church and waved to Emma. "Thanks for coming to get the boys," he said. "I didn't want them wandering the neighborhood."

"I appreciate it," Emma said. "Do you think we'll have our regular meetings tomorrow?"

"I would be surprised if we do," Brother Chappell said. "The cultural hall and chapel are a real mess."

Emma and the kids returned home just as Tad called again. He said the quake had caused more damage in downtown Salt Lake than anywhere else, and that the TRAX train that he usually traveled on wouldn't be running again for the foreseeable future. The earthquake had damaged the tracks in several places.

Emma suddenly felt a little helpless. They only had one car— an aging minivan—and since Tad's office was only a block from one of the TRAX stops, she had the minivan during the day. The arrangement had worked out well—except in this case.

Emma asked, "Do you want me to come pick you up?"

"No, I've found a ride, but it might take a while," Tad said. "The quake buckled part of I-15 near 600 South, and traffic is a mess. Go ahead and eat dinner without me."

"Be careful and hurry home," Emma said. "The boys are excited to tell you about what happened at the Church."

Emma then called her parents in Springville to let them know everyone was safe. They told her the quake had barely been felt in Springville, with just a little shaking.

The Relief Society president then called to let her know that Sunday's meetings had been canceled, and to make sure they were okay. Emma assured her she was fine, but she was saddened to hear that one of their ward members had been critically injured by a falling tree.

Emma fed the kids their dinner early so they could watch the TV news. The quake made the national news programs, and scientists estimated it at 5.7 on the Richter scale, with the epicenter a few miles north of Salt Lake. There was a lot of damage in Bountiful, but the Bountiful Temple was fine, as was Hill Air Force Base a few miles to the north.

The concern among scientists was that while this was a fairly powerful earthquake, it still didn't qualify as "The Big One" along the Wasatch Front that residents had long been awaiting. Everyone would still have to be on guard, especially since this series of tremors over the past year seemed to be growing in intensity.

During the local newscast, the boys cheered when the station showed their damaged church. "We're famous now," Charles said, causing Emma to smile. She was glad they were taking it so well.

When Tad walked in the door about an hour later, he gave each of the kids a hug, then went to Emma and held her tight. "What a day," he said in her ear. "I missed you."

"I missed you, too," she said. "I'm so glad you're safe."

"Well, if we can live through this, we can live through anything," Tad said.

His words were sincere, but little did he know of the epic events that awaited them.

CHAPTER 2

❧

Tad had always been a sports fan, and he had been disappointed when the National Basketball Association—and the Utah Jazz—had folded for financial reasons. He still followed the National Football League closely, rooting for the teams that had former BYU stars playing for them. Also, he had begun to play a new sport called Conquest a couple of years earlier with some of the men in the ward.

The game was an exciting combination of rugby and Ultimate Fighting, set within a huge maze the size of a basketball court. It really got the players' hearts pumping, even if they did get a little beaten up.

Soon Tad was playing Conquest every Saturday in an organized league. It was a lot of fun for spectators to watch as well, and Conquest quickly became popular across the nation.

Within a year, the formation of a professional Conquest league was announced. Most of the owners of the former NBA teams still owned their arenas, and they were desperate to find a way to make some money and fill those empty seats. They saw how Conquest would easily fit on the old basketball courts.

Many analysts had said the NBA folded because the game wasn't violent enough to keep up with pro football. Major league baseball was also struggling for the same reason—fans wanted to see collisions and non-stop action. Conquest certainly met those requirements, and then some. Plus, the owners promoted the matchups more like professional wrestling or boxing, where the top team could be toppled at any time and a new team would be crowned the champion. So there wasn't a regular season like in other sports, but an unending round-robin tournament that continued all year round. It helped create maniacal fanbases and made every game important, because even the weakest teams could win a few games in a row and work their way into a title game.

Some skeptics called it the Hulk Hogan League in honor of the professional wrestler from the 1980s who seemingly won and lost his championship belt every other month in order to keep the fans coming back. There was some truth to that claim, but the owners didn't mind as the fans packed the arenas for every game.

In later years, Conquest's rules would become much more depraved, even leading to occasional deaths. But even in its original version, it was the most violent game the United States had ever seen, and the American public made it the highest-rated sports league in TV history.

Tad had been elated when Salt Lake City was awarded one of the league's franchises. The team would play in the newly renamed Conquest Center, formerly the EnergySolutions Arena.

The Salt Lake Tribune sponsored a contest to name the new team. The contest winner would receive two free season tickets. When Tad heard about the contest, he asked Emma to help him think up a name. She shrugged. "I think you're devoting way too much time to Conquest as it is," she said. "It seems so barbaric. I'm worried someone is going to get killed."

"It's not barbaric," Tad said angrily. "It's the most exciting game ever invented. Plus, it's helping me lose weight."

Emma shot him a fierce look. "You come home with your arms and face bloodied! I'm embarrassed when you go to church with a bandaged forehead. I feel like you and your friends are nothing more than modern-day gladiators."

Tad's face lit up, completely ignoring the tone of Emma's comments. "That's it! The Salt Lake Gladiators," he said. "Can I use that name in the contest?"

Emma rolled her eyes. "Be my guest."

Tad went to the computer and called up the *Tribune*'s website. As he was entering in the suggested name, he said, "How about Gladiatorzz—you know, with two z's—in memory of the Jazz?"

"That sounds fine," Emma said, a bit tired of hearing about Conquest.

A week later, all Emma could do was shake her head when Tad's team name was actually chosen. The team's owners invited him to attend the name unveiling at the Conquest Center, where he would be awarded two season tickets on the front row.

"This is going to be the best day of my life," Tad said.

"Better than our marriage day—or the birth of our children?" Emma asked.

"You're right. I guess it only ranks somewhere in the top five," he responded with a smile.

All in all, it did turn out to be a very memorable day. Tad got his photo taken with all of the team members posing as if they were going to attack him, and the photo appeared on the front page of the *Tribune*'s sports section. It was later made into a life-size banner that hung outside the entrance to the arena.

Tad started painting his face for the games and taunting the other teams, and the TV cameras would naturally focus in on him during timeouts. The commentators started calling him "The Tadinator," and he briefly became a minor celebrity in the Salt Lake area.

The whole situation was rather disturbing to Emma. Her husband had been a quiet accountant for the first fifteen years of their marriage, and now she was sharing him with the whole Salt Lake sports community.

Tad assured her it was all in good fun. "It's better than having me go through a mid-life crisis, isn't it?"

"That's the problem," she said. "I think you *are*."

He laughed at her comment. "Don't worry, I'm already getting a little tired of it," he said. "But I'm enjoying the ride!"

David and Charles enjoyed the extra attention they received

from kids at school for being the Tadinator's sons, and the men at church thought it was hilarious. Nevertheless, Emma made sure the TV was never turned on while Tad was at the games.

One night in early December, Emma's brother Doug gave her a call. "I thought you might want to know that Josh Brown has been called as a mission president," he said.

"Wow, isn't he a little young for that?" Emma asked. Doug's brother-in-law was definitely rising through the ranks of Church leadership, having already served as a bishop and in a stake presidency, but this new calling was a surprise.

"Josh said his call came because of an emergency situation," Doug said. "The president of the Guatemala Quetzaltenango Mission died suddenly two weeks ago, and Josh has been called by the First Presidency to fill the vacancy. He was set apart yesterday, and they'll be leaving for Guatemala soon. We invited them to go to dinner with us tomorrow night, and we all wanted you and Tad to join us."

"Yes, we'd like to come," Emma said. "I'll double-check with Tad, but we should be able to be there. Where are we eating?"

"Let's meet at the Brick Oven at seven."

"Sounds good. We'll see you then."

The next night Tad and Emma left David in charge of the kids and met the other two couples at the Brick Oven Restaurant in Provo. Doug mentioned that he had offered to take the Browns anywhere they wanted, but Josh said he wanted to fill up on a good Brick Oven pizza one last time before departing for Central America.

They all met in the restaurant lobby and soon were seated. The three couples had gotten together for dinner several times over the years, and they were able to easily converse about their lives like hardly any time had passed. But on this night, Emma looked around at the group of friends and smiled to herself. When they had first begun hanging out together during their college days, all three women had worn their hair long. Now they each had short, easily managed hairstyles that fit their busy schedules. Kim's hair had stayed blonde all of these years, and Becky was still a brunette, but Emma's hair had steadily darkened from sandy blonde to dark brown.

The men meanwhile, were also a contrast. Emma had to admit that Tad looked the most youthful, keeping his hair a little longer. Josh's once-dark hair was now cut short and flecked with gray, while her brother Doug really didn't have any hair left! People would sometimes suggest that he shave his head, but he would tell them with a smile, "I'm going to age gracefully."

After the couples had spent a few minutes in small talk, Kim said, "I wish you could have heard the blessing Josh received when he was set apart. The Spirit was so strong in the room. Josh, tell them about it."

Josh kind of waved her off, a little embarrassed. "No, you go ahead," he said.

Kim nodded. "It really was special—and a little overwhelming. It sounds like we will help the missionaries bring many people into the Church, but that we'll also help gather the Saints there and prepare them for great worldwide changes."

"You'll be living next to the new Quetzaltenango Temple, right?" Becky asked. "That will be exciting."

"Yes, it is a special place," Josh said. "In my blessing, the prophet mentioned that we were going to serve among the descendants of the Nephite prophets, and that the blessings promised them in the Book of Mormon were about to be fulfilled."

Tad felt goose bumps go down his back. "Do you really think we're getting that close to the Second Coming?" he asked. "It sometimes seems this old world will always stay the same."

"I think it is closer than we realize," Josh said. "Hopefully we'll all get to be a part of it somehow."

"I'm just grateful we already know the language," Kim said. "My parents are loving their mission in Peru, and so it is a real blessing for us to be able to serve, too. It's been hard not to have children, but now we'll be the parents to more than 150 missionaries!"

Josh laughed. "She makes it sound so easy. When I married Kim and started learning Spanish, I didn't think it would lead to this!"

"What are you going to do with your law practice?" Tad asked.

Josh shrugged. "I'm basically turning my clients over to my partners. I suppose I'll pick up where I left off when we get back."

"I admire you," Tad said. "That's a lot to give up."

"Well, I think you would do the same thing. But the prophet didn't really give me much wiggle room to say no," Josh said. "It will be a fun adventure, to say the least. But I guess the thing I'll miss the most is watching the Tadinator on TV."

He gave Tad a playful punch in the arm, and they all had a good laugh about Tad's alter ego.

⚜ ⚜ ⚜

After the meal, the Norths gave the other couples fond hugs good-bye and wished the Browns well on their new assignment. As they pulled onto I-15, Tad suggested they visit his grandfather, Charles North, who lived in Orem. He and Tad had grown particularly close during Tad's time at BYU, and Emma had grown so fond of him that she had insisted they name their second son after him.

They hadn't seen him in about a month, and when he opened the door, they were stunned by his gaunt face. "Grandpa, I must say you've looked better," Tad said.

"Really? I thought that dropping a few pounds would really help my appearance," he said with a grin. "Actually, I'm glad you stopped by. I've been meaning to talk to you. I've been having some stomach pains, and the doctor gave me some tests last week."

Grandpa North motioned them inside the house, and they sat on the couch while he took a seat in his recliner. Once they were settled, Tad asked, "Did they find your stomach problem?"

"He's pretty sure it's cancer."

"Whoa. I don't know what to say," Tad said. "Are you going to get chemotherapy?"

Grandpa North shook his head. "I don't think I'll be getting any treatments."

"Why not?" Emma asked in surprise.

"Maybe I'm just being stubborn, but the government has a plan that I don't want any part of," he said. "As an old Navy vet, the government always paid my medical bills, so in exchange they think I should be part of a new program they are working on. They're willing to give me chemotherapy at no cost, but they also want to implant a microchip in me."

"A microchip?" Tad asked. "Where would they put it? In your brain?"

Grandpa North laughed. "That might actually help my mental capacity, but no, they want to put it in the back of my right hand. The government has kept this project pretty quiet. They're starting with people like me who are dependent on the government, but the rumor is that they'll want everyone to get chip implants."

"You're kidding! I certainly don't want one," Emma said. "I've heard of chips being put in pets to help identify them if they get lost, but I don't think humans need them."

"Well, neither do I, but they're saying it's the wave of the future," Grandpa North said. "I would be able to pass my hand over a scanner, and the chip would immediately tell a computer all of my medical information. The chip can also contain other items, such as a person's financial history. They say you could even pay bills with it."

"That sounds too intrusive," Tad said. "But the government won't pay your medical bills unless you help test it?"

"That's right. I'm kind of stuck in the middle. I do support my country and I can see how this chip might make everyday life go more smoothly, but it just doesn't feel right. It's too much like Big Brother watching my every move."

"What is this world coming to?" Emma asked, feeling annoyed.

Grandpa North shrugged. "I can see the government's reasons for wanting it. Identity theft and computer fraud are becoming so common that the chip might be the only way to protect our financial assets. The wealthiest citizens are so tired of being victimized that they are really behind the chip, and their lobbyists are pressuring the government to go forward with it. On paper, it sounds like a good idea."

Emma shook her head. "That seems to be going too far. It still doesn't feel right to implant something in your body simply to protect your money."

"Their arguments are pretty solid," Grandpa North replied. "The FBI claims it could make crime nearly nonexistent. The chip would be linked to the GPS tracking system, so the police could capture any suspect simply by tracing the location of his chip. I could see large corporations liking it. For example, when someone calls in to use a sick day, his boss could easily check if the employee is out playing a round of golf when he is supposedly home in bed."

"Why haven't we heard more about this?" Tad asked. "You'd think people would want to know about it."

"It is already being used by private companies in Europe," Grandpa North said. "There's a dance club in France that gives their regular guests a big discount if they use their chip to purchase meals. So it has been proven to work."

"I don't see how they'll force people to take the chip, though," Emma said. "I certainly don't want some chip bulging out of my skin."

"You would hardly notice it was there," Grandpa North said. "They use a little gun-like tool that implants it under the skin and you're as good as new."

"Don't you think the religious groups across the country will oppose it?" Tad asked.

Grandpa North smiled sadly. "The government has already worked out ways to halt any opposition. Just watch. I'll bet

Americans will soon be having them implanted voluntarily."

Emma couldn't believe her ears. "Voluntarily? I really doubt that would happen."

"The doctor that I've been seeing says the government is preparing to put a positive spin on it," Grandpa North said. "They think it will even boost consumer spending. One plan is to give a $2,000 tax credit to anyone who receives a chip in the first 30 days after its introduction. Don't you think most people would jump at the chance to get a lot of money for simply having chips put in the backs of their hands? It will be under the skin and hardly noticeable. Imagine a family of six. That's $12,000 right there."

"I see what you mean," Tad said, a bit discouraged. "When you tell me I could get $10,000 for us and the kids, it could change my mind."

Emma glared at her husband. "Don't even think about it."

"Don't worry," Tad told her. "I don't plan on it."

Tad then proceeded to give Grandpa North a wonderful priesthood blessing, encouraging him to follow the promptings of the Holy Ghost when it came to dealing with his doctor and the government.

After the blessing, Grandpa North had tears in his eyes. "Thank you," he said. "I'm not going to get the chip, even if it costs me my life."

CHAPTER 3

Emma and the kids spent New Years Day putting away the Christmas decorations before the kids had to go back to school the next day. Tad was gone attending a special afternoon Gladiatorzz game at the Conquest Center, but he expected to be home by dinnertime, and he said he would bring pizza home for them.

Without dinner to cook, Emma settled on the couch to watch the evening news, and a commercial came on featuring an attractive young couple in a park. The couple began hugging and kissing, then the man on the screen told the woman, "There's something different about you. You seem more alive than ever."

The woman gave him a confident smile. "It's because I got the chip. You need to get the chip, too."

The couple kissed passionately again before the woman turned to the camera and said softly, "Get the chip."

Emma bolted out of her chair. "Grandpa North was right. The government is starting to push the chip."

During every commercial break throughout the rest of the night there was a 15-second variation of that first chip commercial. The ads didn't give any real explanation about the chip, but they certainly left viewers with a desire to find out about it.

When Tad arrived home, Emma told him about the chip commercials, and he watched several of them. He noted that each commercial targeted a different segment of the population just right.

"Parents, do you know where your kids are? Get the chip, and you always will!"

21

"Don't be a victim of identify theft. The chip makes sure that your identity stays with you!"

"Are you tired of fiddling with clumsy debit cards? Get the chip, and you'll never worry about cash or credit cards again."

"I just got my drivers license, but I don't need to carry it with me. Who needs to worry about a wallet when you've got the chip?"

As the days passed, the commercials gave small clues about the chip. In one advertisement a voice said, "No more papers to sign, no more waiting for your loan to be approved. Get the chip." Then it showed a man in a business suit walk into a car dealership, swipe his hand over a scanner, and then drive away in a new sports car. At the end of the commercial, he leaned out of the car window and pumped his fist excitedly before shouting, "Get the chip!"

Soon the whole nation was talking about the chip. Most people didn't have a clue what it was, but they knew they wanted one!

The following week the ads began to play parts of a new song that was being played on the radio. Tad heard it twice during a single trip to the store. The song had a catchy synthesizer rhythm and consisted of only a few words. Over and over an electronic voice sang, "It's hip to get the chip, yeah, yeah. Do it right, and don't get left behind. It's hip to get the chip!"

When the song ended, the DJ said, "That's the new smash hit 'Get the Chip' by the group Chippy and Friends. It's a stupid name for a group, but that song is awesome!"

Within two days a music video for the song began airing. The video featured "Chippy," a square computer-animated microchip with arms, legs, eyes and a mouth. He was muscular and the size of a human.

In the video, Chip was at a dance club hanging out with a group of famous professional athletes. Beautiful, scantily clad women would approach the group and completely ignore the sports stars. Instead, the women fought for Chip's undivided attention.

The video ended with Chip singing on stage with some of the nation's biggest music stars, dancing a choreographed routine and singing, "It's hip to get the chip!"

"That's the dumbest video I've ever seen," Emma said. "The fact that such a terrible song is so popular is proof that Satan is behind this. I'll bet it has subliminal messages."

Tad shook his head sadly. "With or without Satan's help, that song is going to be huge. The beat is almost hypnotic."

Tad was right. The song shot straight to No. 1 on the Billboard Hot 100 chart, and it became the most downloaded song ever on Apple's iTunes.

Soon people were doing the video's choreographed dance at clubs all across the nation. Music historians noted that there hadn't been a dance sensation this big since "The Macarena" drove everyone crazy in the mid-1990s.

However, despite all of the "Chipmania" invading every aspect of popular culture for several weeks, there still hadn't been an explanation about what the chip actually was.

Then one Sunday night there were news bulletins that the president of the United States would explain more about the chip during a special broadcast the following evening, which fittingly was Presidents Day.

The next day the Norths finished up Family Home Evening and then sent the kids to their rooms early. Emma didn't want them hearing about the chip program until she knew the details herself. So Emma and Tad watched, along with the rest of the nation, as the president outlined everything that Grandpa North had told them a few weeks earlier, including the $2,000 tax incentive.

The president then said, "As we celebrate this special holiday, I believe our noble presidents George Washington and Abraham Lincoln would have welcomed such an innovative technology if it had been available in their times. This microchip is going to improve our lives in every way."

The president explained that "chip implant centers" had been established in all major cities, and that implantation was free through the end of February, along with the tax incentive. Those who waited beyond the end of the month would have to pay an implantation fee and would lose the tax incentive.

The president ended the broadcast by saying, "This program will boost our economy, reduce crime, and make our lives much more efficient. It is a 10-second procedure that only stings a little. I know, because I received the chip myself earlier today." He held up his right hand, and the camera zoomed in on it. The president pointed to a tiny puncture on the back of his hand.

"See, it is hardly noticeable," he said. "As a nation, what have we got to lose?"

Emma went to bed with a sick feeling, sensing the nation had everything to lose.

The next few days were a unique time in America. Each night the TV news would show long lines of people at the chip implant centers, but everyone seemed very upbeat. "Thank you, Mr. President," was a common phrase heard as the TV reporters interviewed the people in line. Even small children seemed excited about getting the chip. A reporter asked one little boy, "What are you going to do with the money?"

"I'm going to Disneyland!" the boy shouted. His mother nodded happily and added, "We have never been able to afford the trip, but our tax rebate will make it possible. God bless America!"

The federal government had been working quietly for months, making sure that each citizen's personal information was ready to be accessed from a computer network that was available at all of the implant centers. A technician simply called up a person's electronic file on the computer, and then after the person was fingerprinted and had verified their identity through two forms of identification, they received the chip. The newest "Flash" technology allowed each chip to hold up to 7 gigabytes of data—enough to easily hold a person's vital information.

The procedure was so fast and easy that people commented that they had never seen a government agency work so fast. One man being interviewed said, "It took me almost two hours to renew my drivers license last month at the Division of Motor Vehicles, so I expected a long wait. But I was done here in 15 minutes."

Most retail stores were quickly equipped with chip scanners, and the government estimated that nearly 40 percent of residents along the East Coast had received the chip in the first four days. Most companies had offered their employees a day off so they could get the chip. The implant centers were staying open 24 hours a day to meet the demand and make it possible for all Americans to receive the chip by the end of the month.

Chip recipients were given the option to have their $2,000 tax rebate deposited directly into their new "chip accounts" rather than waiting to claim the money on their tax return. Naturally, nearly everyone selected to receive—and spend—the newfound money immediately. The media reported that consumer confidence in the economy had reached new heights. Stores could hardly keep their shelves stocked.

Tad and Emma nervously watched the nightly national news broadcasts, which praised the president's plan, and reported that economists were optimistic that the country would experience a long-term retail boom.

Those reports were usually followed by negative stories from Utah or Idaho. In one report, a solemn-faced reporter stood in front of a moderately busy Wal-Mart in Orem and spoke in serious tones about how the citizens in the Midwest and Rocky Mountains were lagging far behind other parts of the nation in getting the chip.

On Saturday evening, a mere six days after his previous TV appearance, the U.S. president went on TV again. He spoke of the overwhelming success of the chip program, and then he concluded by looking straight into the TV camera and saying, "I urge the good people in the Rocky Mountains and in our nation's heartland—the very breadbasket of our country—to step up and become part of this great new economic system. The chip will only bring forth positive results for our nation. As you meet together in your various religious congregations tomorrow, be sure to thank God for bringing this economic blessing to our nation."

The Norths didn't sleep very well that night, feeling that despite the president's encouraging words, America was somehow being led down a dangerous path.

The next Sunday was supposed to be a day of celebration for the ward, since their meetinghouse was finally ready to be used again following the earthquake. They had been meeting at another building all this time. But as the members walked into the chapel the next morning, there was a sense of nervousness. The chip program had emerged so quickly that LDS Church leaders hadn't yet publicly commented on the president's plan. The speculation among the members was that something would be said during sacrament meeting.

Emma noticed there were several families in attendance that hadn't been to church in more than a year, including some who didn't hesitate to say they had already received the chip.

After the opening song and prayer, the bishop stood and announced he had received a letter from the First Presidency, and he had been asked to read it to the congregation. The letter was direct and to the point. The First Presidency emphasized the importance of individual agency, but they strongly discouraged receiving the chip, asking the Saints to trust in the Lord and to continue to be diligent in keeping the commandments.

The letter closed by referring to two recent *Ensign* articles that had emphasized the importance of temporal preparedness, including storing food and water, and having cash on hand in case of an emergency where credit cards or ATMs might not work.

As the bishop sat down, the congregation was buzzing, and the talks by an elderly couple who had recently returned from a mission to Nauvoo were largely ignored.

After getting the kids to their Sunday School and Primary classes, Emma and Tad went to their Gospel Doctrine class, thinking it would be good to be among the stalwart members of the ward on such a stressful day. But Emma was shocked at the various conversations going on around her as they waited for the teacher to come into the classroom. Each person seemed to have his or her own interpretation of the First Presidency's letter:

"Well, it sounded like we are free to do what we feel is best, and we could sure use the money to fix up the house after the earthquake."

"I heard the chip will soon come in different colors so you can actually see it under the skin. That will be cool."

"The letter was no surprise to me. It shows the General Authorities are more behind the times than ever. It is disappointing that with all of this new economic growth, the only thing they can talk about is food storage! And now that we have the chip, why would we need cash?"

"Do you think we need to pay tithing on the tax incentive?"

"I think the best way to follow the prophet is to get the chip so we can stock up on our food storage."

After hearing that last comment, Emma couldn't help herself. She stood up and said loudly, "Did everyone miss the point? The First Presidency said to not get the chip!"

The group turned and looked at her. Emma could tell a few members of the class agreed with her, but most of them had already rationalized the First Presidency's letter. A counselor in the Relief Society presidency called out, "Sister North, the letter never said, 'Do not get the chip.' So don't start preaching to us. That money will bless our lives."

Other members quickly made similar comments, and Emma knew she wouldn't win this fight. So she simply asked the group, "Have you prayed about it?"

She then took Tad's hand, and they left the class. Once they were in the hall, she said to him, "Why didn't you defend me?"

Tad frowned. "Did you have to make a scene? You already knew that most of them would feel that way."

Emma felt like a dagger had been thrust into her heart. "I don't care about what they think. What matters to me is that we do the right thing."

Tears came to her eyes. Tad tried to put a hand on her shoulder, but she pulled away. "I suddenly have a bad headache. I'm walking home," she said. "Please find the kids after church."

She walked out of the building feeling dismayed and betrayed. It was a beautiful sunny day, but Emma felt an uneasiness creep into her soul. She went straight to the side of her bed and spent the next two hours on her knees, praying for guidance and comfort, but the uneasy feeling never went away.

As she heard the door finally open when her family arrived, she closed her prayer by turning the matter over to the Lord, saying, "Heavenly Father, help me get through whatever awaits us."

Tad came into the bedroom and put his arms around her. "I'm sorry," he said. "You just caught me off guard in the class."

Emma hugged him back. "I know. I was just furious at what they were saying. You agree with me, don't you?"

"Of course," Tad said. "You know how I feel about the chip."

By the middle of March, Americans could use the chip to access almost anything. Cash was quickly becoming a nuisance. Grocery cashiers acted highly inconvenienced to even open the cash drawer. Most places still accepted credit cards, but a simple 30-second transaction now felt cumbersome and time-consuming when compared to using the chip.

On Emma's most recent trip to the grocery store, she noticed a new checkout line with a sign that read, "*Chip Express Lane.*" She watched as at least a dozen people zoomed though the line as fast as their groceries could be bagged. Meanwhile, the line she was in crept along slowly.

The woman standing in front of her grew exasperated. "This wait is ridiculous," she said. "I'm getting chipped tonight."

Within another month, many gas stations were "Chip only." School districts across the nation asked that children who were going to eat school lunch be "chipped" before the new school year began.

"What are you going to do for our kids, pack lunches for them every day?" Tad asked.

"It looks like I'll have to," Emma said. "By the way, a couple of other moms have talked about starting a home-school group. What do you think?"

"Wouldn't that be a lot of trouble?"

"I don't care," Emma said. "I am not going to let my kids get the chip."

From the next room Leah innocently started to sing, "It's hip to get the chip. Yeah, yeah."

Emma could hardly believe her ears. "Don't sing that song in our home!" she called out.

Leah came into the room. "Why not?" she asked. "The kids sing it during recess."

"That doesn't make it right," Emma said. "We aren't getting the chip."

CHAPTER 4

⸎

Josh and Kim's first month in Guatemala had been a whirlwind of meetings and attending baptisms. They had moved into the mission home near the recently completed Quetzaltenango Guatemala Temple but had spent most of their time visiting each of the mission's zones and getting to know their missionaries.

The city of Quetzaltenango, where the Browns lived, was the second largest city in Guatemala. The city and its nearby villages filled a valley that had been formed by ten surrounding volcanoes, one of which continued to send volcanic dust into the air every few days.

Quetzaltenango had always been plagued by a lack of urban planning and poorly constructed dwellings, and that situation had worsened as thousands of people had come down from the mountains in recent years. Jobs for the newcomers were scarce, and portions of the valley were now filled with poverty and hopelessness. The people had been oppressed in some way seemingly since the Spanish explorers first arrived in the 1500s and completely disrupted their way of life.

Despite the widespread poverty, the Browns found delightful people in every area throughout the mission. These Saints were very poor in material possessions, but they radiated the light of the gospel. The mission consisted of more than 20 stakes, and each stake presidency consisted of homegrown Guatemalans, most of whom had served missions themselves in the United States or elsewhere.

Most of these leaders had become successful businesspeople

with the help of the Perpetual Education Fund initiated by President Gordon B. Hinckley in the 1990s. The fund had provided student loans that had allowed these men and women to receive a better education than they could have ever imagined. Now a quarter of a century later, the fruits of that program had blossomed in amazing ways as the children of those original participants were also receiving schooling with the help of the fund. Latter-day Saints were very influential in every aspect of Guatemalan life.

The Browns had been surprised to discover that there weren't any American-born missionaries in their mission. Every missionary under their jurisdiction was a native of Guatemala. This trend had become commonplace in recent years throughout the world where enough homegrown missionaries were available. People who were interested in the Church just seemed more comfortable learning the gospel from someone who had grown up in similar circumstances as they had.

In fact, the past two mission presidents had been natives of Guatemala, so everyone thought it was funny that these American "gringos" were now here. Josh humorously mentioned it whenever they greeted a new congregation, saying, "Sister Brown and I are very happy to be here. We feel we can learn something new from each of you. So all we ask is that you just love us, and we'll love you back. We promise to behave at least as well as the first Spaniards did when they visited your ancestors."

That comment would always bring a laugh from the group and break the ice. Then Josh would bear a powerful testimony of the Book of Mormon and the truthfulness of the gospel.

The missionaries immediately looked to Josh as their spiritual leader. The work surged forward, with hundreds of baptisms taking place each week. Josh had to assign an extra set of missionaries to the mission office just to keep up with the paperwork.

Kim was particularly delighted by the bright, colorful clothing of the people. She was given a pair of traditional Mayan dresses by an elderly sister, and she wore them whenever the occasion permitted, which endeared her to the members.

Kim was especially intrigued by the success the missionaries were having with the native Mayan communities in the Guatemalan highlands. Soon after they had arrived, Kim traveled to one of these distant areas and spent a weekend as a "third companion" with two sister missionaries who had both grown up in Guatemala.

One of the sisters, Sister Silva, had actually graduated from BYU before her mission. She was able to tell Kim many interesting things about the Guatemalan people and the Church's growth there.

As they walked along a dirt road to meet with a family, Kim told Sister Silva, "Before I came here, I read several books that spoke about how the events in the Book of Mormon probably took place right here in this area. Do the Church members here understand that and feel the same way?"

Sister Silva's face brightened. "We certainly do. More than a third of Guatemala's citizens are of pure Mayan descent, while nearly everyone else is a mix of Mayan and Spanish descent. So we believe that we are the descendants the Book of Mormon prophets wrote about who will accept the gospel in the last days and receive many wonderful blessings."

"I guess I hadn't realized the Mayans were still thriving," Kim said. "I always thought they died off centuries ago from disease and battles when the Spaniards arrived."

Sister Silva shook her head. "Some were killed, and some of the lowland cities were destroyed, but most of the Mayans just moved from their cities up into the mountains."

Kim responded, "I must admit I haven't really studied this very much, but I'm curious to know if there have been any discoveries that give evidence the Book of Mormon took place here?"

Sister Silva said, "When I was at BYU, I naturally had an interest in this topic, and I took several classes from professors who specialized in Book of Mormon studies. I was excited to read several of their books that gave strong evidence that the major Book of Mormon events took place in Central America, and the Mayans were likely the descendants of the Book of Mormon people."

Sister Silva's companion, Sister Alvarado, then said, "One of the greatest evidences for me is how the oral traditions that have been passed down for centuries by our families match the stories and teachings that are found in the Bible and the Book of Mormon."

Sister Silva added, "That is true. The Catholic missionaries recognized the Christian similarities many years ago, and it helped convert most of our ancestors to Christianity. I think their teachings helped prepare our people for the restored gospel."

They arrived at the investigator family's doorstep, and Kim put her arms around both missionaries. "Thank you for letting me come with you. I feel I am working with true angels."

The sisters smiled at her, and the trio spent the next hour teaching another wonderful family about the Church.

About two months after their arrival, Josh received a phone call from the Church's Area President. He said, "We have been notified that Elder Smith of the Quorum of the Twelve will be traveling through Guatemala next week, and he will be holding a special meeting for all of the stake presidencies in the Quetzaltenango region. The meeting will be in the temple on Saturday at 1 p.m., and he has asked that you and Sister Brown be in attendance."

"We'll be there," Josh said.

Then the Area President added, "There's one other thing. He wants to meet privately with both of you for a few minutes before that meeting."

"Okay, but do you have any idea why?"

"Nope," the Area President said with a chuckle. "I wish you the best of luck!"

For the next few days, Josh and Kim tried to pretend the meeting wouldn't be very important, although they sensed something of greater proportions was going to happen.

"I'm sure this is just a routine evaluation of the mission, since we are new," Josh told Kim.

The Browns had deeply admired Elder Smith ever since his call to the apostleship, although they hadn't ever met him. He had been in the Quorum of the Twelve for only two years and was still the quorum's junior member, but he had brought a youthful, dynamic personality to the calling. His ability to speak fluent Spanish was also a big plus, and Church members in Spanish-speaking countries had embraced him wholeheartedly.

On the appointed day, the Browns waited at the temple doors with other local Church leaders. The apostle had spent the night in Guatemala City, and had departed early that morning to make the four-hour drive to the Quetzaltenango Temple. When his car pulled up outside the temple, Kim's anxiety level reached new heights.

Elder Smith quickly exited the car and kindly greeted the temple presidency. Then he looked past them to the American couple standing behind the group.

"President and Sister Brown, I presume?" the apostle asked.

"Yes, we are," Josh said.

Elder Smith stepped forward and shook hands with both of them. "Let's go find a quiet room inside," he said.

The temple president escorted them to his office, and the apostle told him, "Give us about a half hour."

Elder Smith shut the door and then took a seat behind the desk, motioning for Josh and Kim to sit in the chairs before him. Once they were situated, the apostle sat quietly, looking straight into Josh's eyes. He got right to the point. "President Brown, are you living a clean and virtuous life?"

"I am."

"Is there anything in your life that would prevent me from issuing you any calling in the Church?"

"Do you mean in addition to the one I've already got?" Josh asked, feeling a little overwhelmed.

The apostle smiled. "Just answer the question."

"No, there isn't anything that would prevent me from accepting any calling. I feel more in tune with the Lord than I ever have."

Elder Smith looked at Kim. "Do you agree with your husband's assessment of his life?"

"I do," Kim said. "He is a righteous man."

The apostle nodded. "Then we can continue. President Brown, the Lord has selected you to be a member of the First Quorum of the Seventy. As you know, a calling to this quorum typically means you will serve for the rest of your life—or at least until retirement age, so you have many years ahead of you! It will alter your life in many ways, but I know you will be richly blessed. Do you accept this calling from the Lord?"

Josh's jaw dropped. "I . . . I . . . do."

"Very well. Next month you will travel to Salt Lake and be sustained in General Conference. While you are there you will be ordained to your new calling, and you can tie up any loose ends you might have in the United States. Then you will return here. Guatemala will be your home for the foreseeable future. I would advise you to sell your home in Utah, and transfer all of your financial assets here for use in building up the Lord's kingdom."

Josh and Kim turned to look at each other, both stunned at this news. "So am I still the mission president?" Josh asked.

"For the time being," Elder Smith answered. "Sister Brown, you will be at your husband's side through all of his assignments."

"Wow, this is quite a shock," Kim said.

The apostle smiled again. "I appreciate your humbleness. The prophet has asked me to share with you some of your upcoming assignments. I ask that you keep this information confidential, but you two have some key roles to play as the Lord's work moves forward and prophecies are fulfilled. To give some background on your assignments, let's first open the scriptures."

Elder Smith pulled his scriptures out of a briefcase, and Josh found copies for Kim and himself on a nearby shelf.

"First of all," the apostle said, "the death of the previous mission president was unfortunate, but let me assure you that it wasn't an accident. I am confident the Lord has work for him to do in the Spirit World, and that you two are meant to be in Guatemala at this time. I dare say that you were foreordained to these positions and to perform the tasks that lie ahead of you."

Josh and Kim sat quietly, not sure how to respond. Elder Smith chuckled a little. "I know this is a lot to throw at you all at once," he said. "Please open the Book of Mormon to the book of Third Nephi. It will explain things more clearly than I can. As you know, this is where the Savior is talking to the Nephites during His visit to them here in the Western Hemisphere after His resurrection, and He is telling the people what would happen to their descendants in the last days. Sister Brown, could you read Third Nephi 21:22-25?"

Kim read, *"But if they will repent and hearken unto my words, and harden not their hearts, I will establish my church among them, and they shall come in unto the covenant and be numbered among this the remnant of Jacob, unto whom I have given this land for their inheritance;*

"And they shall assist my people, the remnant of Jacob, and also as many of the house of Israel as shall come, that they may build a city, which shall be called the New Jerusalem.

"And then shall they assist my people that they may be gathered in, who are scattered upon all the face of the land, in unto the New Jerusalem.

"And then shall the power of heaven come down among them; and I also will be in the midst."

"Thank you," Elder Smith said. "Tell me, President Brown, how much of that prophecy has been fulfilled?"

Josh looked at the verses again. "I would say just the first verse. The Church has been established, and the Nephite descendants are now being numbered with the Saints. But we're still waiting for the time when New Jerusalem will be built."

"That is correct," the apostle said. "Who will build New Jerusalem? Will it be members of the Church?"

"Of course," Josh answered. "My understanding is that the Saints in America will be joined by descendants of the Nephites—the people the Savior is talking to in these verses—and they will work together to build the city."

Kim was a bit puzzled. "So where do we fit into this?"

Elder Smith paused and his eyes actually got a little misty. "The people of this area are descendants of the Book of Mormon prophets," he said. "You will soon have the privilege of leading them to Missouri in preparation to fulfill these prophecies, where the Savior himself will someday be in their midst!"

Kim felt like she was going to faint. Josh was feeling a little weak, too. "How do we even start?" he asked.

"We are still in a time of preparation," the apostle said. "But as a member of the First Quorum of the Seventy, you will have the authority to organize and preside over the people. To be honest, we still don't know exactly when it will happen. A lot of it will depend on the situation in the United States, which I'm afraid is deteriorating rapidly. It could be within months, or it might be a year or two, but these people need to be prepared."

Elder Smith continued, "In my meeting with the stake presidents this afternoon, I will encourage them to develop the spirit of consecration. These people are already very loving and kind. As they focus on serving each other and caring for the poor and the needy, they'll also develop the spiritual strength they will need. As I mentioned earlier, we need to keep this conversation to ourselves. The time hasn't come for this people to depart for Missouri, and it wouldn't be beneficial to even hint at what lies ahead for them."

Kim was feeling more dazed by the minute. "But why did the Lord choose us?" she said, looking over at her husband. "Sorry, Josh. I love you, but I feel we are both completely inadequate."

The apostle laughed. "From small things, great things shall come to pass. You will do fine. I believe you have been prepared for this assignment all of your lives, and you are both great leaders, despite your opinion, Sister Brown."

Kim smiled a little. "I guess what I'm trying to say is with so many talented leaders already here, why were we chosen?"

Elder Smith rubbed his chin thoughtfully. "I think a main reason you two 'gringos' were given this calling is the fact that you know the way to New Jerusalem. I don't think it was an accident that you lived in Kansas for many years and know exactly where Independence, Missouri is. Because of that preparation, you will know which roads to follow and the right landmarks to look for. Even with maps, none of the current leaders here would be able to do that very effectively."

His answer helped Kim a lot. She started to feel a bit calmer. But then a question came to her mind. "What about the rest of the Nephite descendants?" Kim asked. "Surely there are millions of Saints all over Central and South America that also qualify for these blessings. Will they all gather to Missouri?"

"No," the apostle said. "Keep in mind that the scripture says only a 'remnant' will return to New Jerusalem. So not everyone will be called upon to return to help build the New Jerusalem—only a small portion."

"Then where will everyone else go?" Kim asked.

"The Saints throughout the Western Hemisphere, from Canada to Chile, will soon be told to take shelter in mountain camps or other protected places during a time of worldwide difficulties. After the danger has passed, the Saints will gather to their nearest temple and build up a Zion community around it," Elder Smith said. "This is in fulfillment of Joseph Smith's prophecy that the Church will fill North and South America. New Jerusalem will simply be the central city of Zion, with hundreds of so-called 'sister cities' built across the world in preparation for the Millennium."

"Wow, that's amazing," Josh said.

The apostle nodded. "In the Doctrine and Covenants the Lord tells the Saints to 'stand in holy places.' That can have a spiritual meaning, but it is also literal. The Lord's people will gather at His temples."

He continued, "It wasn't an accident that President Hinckley accelerated the building of temples during his presidency. We needed to prepare gathering places for the Saints. These temples will eventually be the centerplaces in cities of Zion. Wherever possible, this will happen all over the world, with Saints building beautiful communities in preparation for the Savior's Second Coming."

Josh shook his head in wonder. "I have never even thought of it in that magnitude!"

"But what about the destructions that are supposed to happen?" Kim asked. "Section 45 of the Doctrine and Covenants has always scared me a little."

"There are always going to be trials in this world, and the Lord has said that the wicked will reap their reward," Elder Smith said. "So yes, there are likely going to be some major changes take place, particularly in the United States. This is mainly to allow a situation that will allow New Jerusalem to be built. But trust in the Lord. He will watch over the Saints."

"So we're getting close to the end, aren't we?" Josh asked.

"Let me put it this way," the apostle said. "It has taken almost 200 years for the Church to reach this stage, both financially and spiritually, but now we are ready to dramatically step forward and bless the lives of millions of people. This is all in preparation for the return of our Savior and King. The Second Coming won't happen for a few years, but yes, we are getting close!"

The three sat in silence for a few moments as the Spirit strongly testified to them of the truthfulness of what they had discussed. They stood and embraced each other, and then Elder Smith chuckled a little.

"I need to let you know that if someone comes along soon and volunteers to give you a hand, don't hesitate to accept his help," the apostle said. "I know that the Lord will be sending an angel to help you complete your tasks, but he will likely be wearing blue jeans and work gloves rather than white robes. So be on the lookout for him!"

CHAPTER 5

❖

Back in Salt Lake City, Tad was deep in thought as the TRAX train took him to work. The chip seemed to be dividing the Church. Despite the strong letters and talks from the General Authorities against the chip, many members had gone ahead and received it. They seemed no worse for the wear, and some seemed to be prospering more than before.

Tad shook his head in frustration. When he first heard about the chip, he was completely against it. He was certain it was the so-called "Mark of the Beast" spoken of in the Bible. But as the days rolled by, he wasn't so sure. Tad kept waiting to hear of anyone being disciplined by the Church for getting the chip, but so far he hadn't heard of anybody getting in trouble for doing so.

There was also a rumor going around that people with home mortgages would need to receive the chip to track their loan payments, or else they would have to pay off the balance. If that policy went into effect, he would never be able to buy a home.

"The ward members who chose not to follow the prophet seem to be making more money than ever before," he muttered to himself. "I can barely afford a three-bedroom apartment."

Tad did have hope that his company president, Ken Turner, would stand strong against the government's efforts to implement the chip into their company. Ken was an active member of the Church, and he had spoken out against the chip from the beginning.

Besides, their accounting firm was one of the first new tenants in the Church's beautiful new City Creek Center business complex to the south of Temple Square, and Tad was certain that the Church would encourage its tenants to avoid using the chip.

The following Monday morning as Tad settled into his cubicle, he noticed a memo on his desk that there was a mandatory staff meeting at 9:30 a.m. A co-worker soon passed by and said, "I think the meeting has something to do with the chip."

Tad nervously watched the clock creep forward, then he went to the meeting a little early to talk to Ken, but he hadn't arrived yet. Once all the employees were in the room, Ken finally entered and stood at the end of the room. He looked completely exhausted and beaten down. His hair had seemingly gone gray over the weekend. He fumbled with some papers in his hands, and didn't make eye contact with anyone.

"I appreciate everyone coming here on such short notice," Ken said. "We all know how the business world has been revolutionized by the introduction of the chip. We have carefully weighed our options and have decided to join other companies across the nation by implementing chip scanners for our day-to-day operations, particularly for payroll purposes. Any employees who don't receive the chip by the end of the pay period in two weeks will likely have their paychecks delayed—or maybe they just won't get paid!"

The group laughed. Most of the employees weren't members of the Church, and nearly all of them had already received the chip.

Ken gave a smile and then said, "Well, let's get back to earning those paychecks!"

The employees filed out, but anxiously Tad waited for Ken to pass by. "Can I talk to you for a moment?" he asked.

"Certainly," Ken said. "Come into my office. I thought you might have a question or two."

Once they were seated in Ken's office, Tad asked, "As an active member of the Church, how do you justify this?"

Ken smiled sadly. "This was a very difficult decision for me— until the board of directors said they would fire me if I didn't comply. I had to put my family first. I have two sons on missions right now. If I lose my job, how would I support them? Plus, I'm in the bishopric, and how would the ward members feel if I lost my job and had to use fast-offering money to feed my family? As you know, the government now won't even process a person's unemployment benefits without the chip."

"Even then, I still don't think I can do it," Tad said. "This isn't a money issue, it's a moral issue."

Ken stood and went to his office window that overlooked the City Creek Center's beautiful outdoor gardens. "Tad, look at this wonderful area the Church has built to keep businesses here in downtown Salt Lake. Do you really believe the Church leaders don't realize that billions of dollars are going to be lost if the Church members and their businesses refuse to get the chip? We'll go from being one of the richest churches in the world to one of the poorest."

"There must be a way around it," Tad said. "I can't see the Church giving in for financial reasons."

Ken shook his head. "The costs are too great. If the Church leaders really are going to take a stance against the chip, I feel they are asking too much of us. They'll destroy the Church."

Tad struggled to absorb what he was hearing. He had been sure Ken would be the last person to succumb to the pressure. "So I guess this means you're going to get chipped?" Tad asked.

Ken held out his right hand, and Tad could see a tiny mark. "You've done it already?" he asked.

"I got it on Friday, and I recommend that you do the same," Ken said. "There's no reason to tell Emma. What she doesn't know won't hurt her."

"Wow, I don't want to lie to Emma."

"How is it a lie?" Ken asked. "You do dozens of work-related tasks every day that you don't tell Emma about. Just consider getting the chip to be one of them."

Tad didn't respond, and Ken slapped him on the shoulder. "You have a bright future with this company. I expect at least two of our top employees will leave because of this announcement, and you are in a great position to fill one of their spots. I'll bet you'll double your salary within a year."

Tad was surprised. "Do you really mean that?"

"Definitely. The members of the board of directors have mentioned your name several times. They are impressed with you. Don't throw away this opportunity."

CHAPTER 6

Tad went back to his cubicle. His back muscles tightened up from the stress. He weighed his options, and getting the chip seemed to be the only realistic answer. With one simple procedure, he could guarantee financial security for his family. "I probably wouldn't even notice the chip most of the time," he said to himself.

As he pondered his dilemma, the phone on his desk rang. He checked the caller ID. It was his Grandpa North's number. His grandpa called him occasionally, although this phone call seemed particularly timely.

"Hi, Grandpa," Tad said into the phone, forcing some happiness into his voice. "How is everything?"

There was a brief pause, and then he heard the voice of his father, Roy. "Hi Tad, it's Dad. I'm calling to let you know Grandpa has passed away."

Tad was briefly speechless. He couldn't believe this was coming right on top of the meeting he'd just had about the chip.

"Tad? Are you there?" Roy asked.

"I'm here, Dad. I knew this was coming, but I'm just a little shook up, I guess."

"We all are," Roy said. "I came up from St. George last night to be with him, and when I checked on him this morning, he had died. It looked like he went peacefully in his sleep."

"How can I help?" Tad asked.

"We're going to have the funeral on Wednesday, with the viewing tomorrow night," Roy said. "I hope you can get off work on such short notice."

"I should be able to," Tad said. "I'll go check with my boss right now."

"Good. I'll talk to you tonight."

After hanging up, Tad went to talk to Ken, who was very understanding. "Yes, certainly take the next couple of days off," he said.

"Thank you. My grandpa meant very much to me."

Ken nodded. "When you get back, we can talk more about your future."

During Grandpa North's funeral, Tad felt a bitterness building inside him. The other family members were hailing Grandpa North as a wonderful man—which Tad readily admitted he was—but they were all focusing on his refusal to accept the chip. Over and over he heard, "He died following the counsel of the prophet."

Tad couldn't help thinking, "Well, that's true. But if he had gotten the chip, the government would have paid for his chemotherapy and he would still be with us."

Then Tad would mentally kick himself, knowing his grandpa had stuck to his principles to the very end.

After the graveside service at the Orem City Cemetery, Emma asked if they could drive down to Springville to visit her parents. When they arrived at the house, they saw Emma's brother Doug was also there.

As they entered, Doug was at the kitchen table talking intently with his father Mark. They paused their conversation and offered Tad their condolences about Grandpa North's passing. Then Doug said, "I'm glad you two are here. I was just telling Dad about a project I am helping set up in Hobble Creek Canyon as part of my new calling as the Stake Preparedness Coordinator. I think you two would be interested in what we are doing."

"Tell us about it," Emma said.

"Well, we have been storing tents and supplies in buildings near the Jolley's Ranch campground. I'm not sure of all of the details yet, but I really believe the campground is being prepared as a refuge for Church members in case of a major emergency."

"What kind of emergency?" Tad asked. "We hardly seem to be in a situation to evacuate. The economy is booming right now."

Doug shook his head. "Tad, we both know this economic boom is mainly based on people spending their 'chip money.' What happens when that money is all spent? The economy could easily collapse on itself. And what about those of us who haven't received the chip? We'll be the ones who get shut out by the government if things go bad."

Tad didn't answer immediately, knowing Doug was right. "So what is the plan?" Tad finally asked. "Gather to the mountains?"

"If necessary," Doug said. "The Church is quietly preparing for such an event, and I think at the right time they'll say more about it publicly."

"When will we know it is time to gather?" Emma asked.

Doug shrugged. "I expect the prophet and apostles themselves will direct us, through the proper priesthood channels. The refuge is being prepared under the direction of the Presiding Bishopric, and there are similar refuges being prepared all throughout the West. They are even hauling wheat from people's food storages, collecting tools, and setting up areas for cows and chickens. Each stake will have a gathering place."

Emma let out a sigh of relief. "I'm so glad to hear the Church is looking ahead," she said. "I've been worried about what we would do if things got worse."

Tad felt his bitterness surge again. Even two weeks ago he would have been very interested in these plans, but the combination of his work situation and Grandpa North's death had his mind reeling.

"Let's not get too carried away," Tad said. "Emma, we're going to be fine. All the Church has done for nearly 200 years is scare everyone into thinking a disaster is just around the corner. All I hear is, 'Get your food storage! Get your food storage!' I'm certainly not giving up a good job just to run off with some doomsday group."

Doug shook his head. "I would hardly call the Church a

doomsday group. The General Authorities have been very cautious not to cause a panic among the members of the Church."

"You can look at it however you want," Tad said, "but tell me this, Doug. If you take off into the mountains, who is going to pay your mortgage?"

"That's a good question," Doug said. "I have thought a lot about that. I wish I was like Mom and Dad and had my house paid off, but I don't. But I think if I left my house to join a mountain camp and stopped making payments, the bank would rightfully foreclose on it within a few months. I would be all right with that, because that is the bank's legal right to do so. Then the bank could sell the house at a fair market value and probably get even more money out of it than the amount I owe them."

Tad pondered Doug's response, deep in thought. "Then what about credit card debt?"

"That's why Becky and I have avoided using credit cards, because who knows what the credit card companies would do? With a mortgage, you have a house the bank can take as collateral. But with credit cards, you don't really have any collateral to settle the debt, especially if your house is already taken. I'd hate to be dragged out of a Church camp and thrown into prison simply because of credit card debt. I don't know if it will reach that point, but I could see credit card companies demanding it. What a tragedy that would be."

Tad was listening closely, trying to sort it out in his head. "But don't you think the Church would give everyone enough notice about the camps so members could sell their homes?"

Doug shook his head. "That wouldn't make any sense. There would suddenly be a glut of homes for sale, and people wouldn't get a fair value. It would throw the whole housing market into a tailspin. Don't forget, the Church has already been through this before. When the Saints were given a deadline to leave Nauvoo after Joseph Smith's death, they couldn't get anybody to give them a fair price. Some of the Church leaders couldn't even sell their homes or sold them for ridiculously low prices, because the mobs knew that all they had to do was wait for the Saints to leave, and then they would have the houses for themselves."

Tad frowned. "We live in a different world now. We aren't so uncivilized that people would take someone's house like that."

Doug raised his eyebrows. "Do you really believe that? I feel the exact same thing would happen, except it would be our own unscrupulous members waiting to capitalize on the situation. But you're missing the point. I believe the call to go to the camps will be a test of faith. Will people really be willing to sacrifice their material possessions to follow the prophet? I think fewer people would do it than you would expect."

"So you are saying you would throw away all of the home equity you've built up the past few years?" Tad asked. "And what about your furniture? Would you leave that too?"

"If the prophet asked us to leave quickly, I'd leave everything," Doug said, staring into his brother-in-law's eyes.

Tad looked away. "But what about all the LDS millionaires?" he asked. "I can't see too many of them giving up their fortunes."

"Who do you think bought all of the property for the gathering places?" Doug responded. "In most cases, the refuge properties have been bought by a wealthy LDS member who then gave the land to the Church. The same thing has happened with the purchase of the electric generators and the tents. None of the set-up costs for the refuges are coming out of the Church's tithing fund. The money is coming from private individuals who have been asked by top Church leaders to contribute. If I was a millionaire, I couldn't think of a better way to use my wealth than to help provide refuges for the Lord's people."

Tad shook his head. "Doug, I don't quite believe you. You make it sound like the Church has got this all organized behind the scenes. I have to say I think you're getting fanatical—or even gone a little nuts."

Emma stared at Tad. She didn't quite know what to say. They had discussed similar things in the past and Tad had always been supportive of doing whatever the prophet asked.

Finally Doug said, "Um, Tad, maybe I didn't explain what I meant very well . . ."

"No, it's all right," Tad said. "I'm sorry, I shouldn't have said that about you. I'll go check on the kids."

Tad walked outside, and Doug asked Emma, "Has Tad been talking this way for long?"

Emma was on the verge of tears. "No, but the past couple of days he has been very distant."

"Well, that certainly didn't sound like the brother-in-law I've known for so many years," Doug said. "To be honest, I'm a little worried about him."

"Me too," Emma said.

CHAPTER 7

The Dalton family had recently celebrated the calling of two missionaries in the family. Emma and Doug's parents, Mark and Michelle, had recently been called to serve as full-time work missionaries at the Jolley's Ranch campground in Hobble Creek Canyon east of Springville. The Church had recently bought the entire campground from Springville City, and the Daltons were spending five days a week at the campground with several other older couples to prepare the area for a large group to live there if necessary.

Doug was particularly happy with his parents' callings, because Mark kept him informed on the specific progress being made at the camp. Similar camps were being built by the Church throughout the Rocky Mountains. Some of these camps were currently being used as Boy Scout or Young Women camps, but both Mark and Doug felt the Church was being guided by the Lord for a greater purpose.

One of Mark's missionary duties was to install a self-supporting hydroelectric generator along Hobble Creek that would provide enough power for a small community. He and several other men also constructed a sturdy 12-foot-high metal fence all the way around the entire campground that was almost impossible to cross.

Meanwhile, Michelle helped prepare a communal kitchen area that the Saints would share. She also helped label and organize the containers of food that were being delivered by large trucks each week.

Although there still hadn't been an official announcement about the mountain camps, word began to spread about them through the stakes, and it caused a mixed reaction. A few members felt it was only a matter of time until the Saints would gather together at the camps, but the vast majority felt it was an overreaction. The general mood was, "Why should I go live in a tent when I have a nice home?"

However, in the April General Conference, the prophet and apostles left no doubt that the Saints needed to be prepared for major changes in their lives.

During the Saturday morning session, one apostle explained that while each geographical area of the Church faced different circumstances, members of the Church should be ready if called upon to separate themselves from the world and gather together.

Another apostle spoke about how the Lord always removes his chosen people from a wicked society. He said, "Enoch left a wicked society to build a great city. Moses led the children of Israel out of Egypt. Even Nephi was commanded by the Lord to separate his family from his brothers soon after they arrived in the Americas. We read in Second Nephi 5:5-7:

"And it came to pass that the Lord did warn me, that I, Nephi, should depart from them and flee into the wilderness, and all those who would go with me.

"Wherefore, it came to pass that I, Nephi, did take my family, and also Zoram and his family, and Sam, mine elder brother and his family, and Jacob and Joseph, my younger brethren, and also my sisters, and all those who would go with me, and all those who would go with me were those who believed in the warnings and revelations of God; wherefore, they did hearken unto my words.

"And we did take our tents and whatsoever things were possible for us, and did journey in the wilderness for the space of many days. And after we had journeyed for the space of many days we did pitch our tents."

The apostle then skipped to verse 10 and continued:

"And we did observe to keep the judgments, and the statutes, and the commandments of the Lord in all things. . . .

"And the Lord was with us; and we did prosper exceedingly; for we did sow seed, and we did reap again in abundance. And we began to raise flocks, and herds, and animals of every kind."

He then looked into the TV camera and said, "There are those among us who may soon go through similar circumstances. Eliminate any credit card debt, and live within your means. Set your lives in order so that you could leave your current situation at a moment's notice if the Lord asks. That time may soon come, and you must be free from the world's entanglements."

⁂

Between conference sessions, Tad took Leah for a long walk, and Emma sensed he just didn't want to discuss what had been said by the apostles. Everything they had said fell in line with what Doug had argued about.

Tad and Leah returned in time for the Saturday afternoon session, and Tad seemed perfectly fine. Emma had been praying in her heart all day that the Conference messages would help him see that Doug wasn't just making stuff up about the camps.

While the morning session had been like a thunderclap, the Norths were even more surprised when the names of the Church leaders were read and Josh Brown was announced as a new member of the First Quorum of the Seventy. The camera followed Josh as he took his place among the other General Authorities.

"Wow, I always sensed that such a calling might come to Josh, but not at such a young age," Emma said.

Emma was happy when Tad took David to the Priesthood Session. When they returned home, she asked him what had been said in the meeting.

"It was definitely interesting," Tad said. "The prophet strongly condemned the chip."

However, the climactic moment of General Conference came at the end of the Sunday afternoon session, when the prophet announced that calls for proselyting missions were being indefinitely suspended. No young men or women would be called to serve as full-time missionaries for the foreseeable future, and all U.S.-born missionaries serving outside the United States would be returning home within two weeks. Senior couples who were serving at temples were asked to continue their missions, but all other senior missionaries would be returning home.

David was somber after the announcement. "Will I ever get to serve as a missionary?" he asked.

"I'm sure other ways will come for you to serve," Emma said.

CHAPTER 8

The Browns invited Doug and Becky to attend Josh's ordination as a General Authority the day after General Conference ended. The blessing indicated the Browns would see marvelous events during their lifetimes, and that the Kingdom of God must always come first. They were told if they fulfilled their duties in the Lord's earthly kingdom, they would receive an exalted place in his heavenly kingdom. It was a beautiful experience that left everyone in tears.

Afterward, Josh took Doug aside and said, "I really get the impression that Kim and I will never live again in that house we just bought. I expect to be living in Guatemala for the next while, so I would like you to sell the house for us. Keep a percentage for yourself, and then send the rest to us.""

"We'll be happy to do that for you," Doug said.

Josh then took his sister Becky in his arms. "I honestly don't know when I will see you again," he told her.

She smiled up at him, with tears in her eyes. "I love you, and you've always been such a great example to me. Just keep doing what you're supposed to do!"

The Daltons drove the Browns to the airport. After another round of tearful farewells, the Browns got on a plane, not sure when they would see their loved ones again.

✤ ✤ ✤

When the Browns arrived in Guatemala, they got right back to work. Of course, the Saints were very pleased to have a General Authority living among them, and the missionary work seemed to reach new heights. There were occasions when entire extended families would join the Church within a few weeks of each other. Josh's main responsibility was keeping on top of the growth, and making sure there were priesthood leaders tracking all of the new members.

Each Friday morning Josh would attend an endowment session in the temple. One morning as he walked to the temple, he saw a group of people watching a small TV in a coffee shop. He stopped to see what they were so interested in. There was a weather map on the screen showing the Gulf of Mexico. To the south of Cuba was definitely a hurricane. In the past, hurricanes had devastated parts of Guatemala, and any hint of an approaching storm was taken very seriously.

"Isn't it pretty early in the year for a hurricane?" Josh asked a man in a business suit. "It's only the end of April."

"Yes, but there it is," the man said. "Hurricane Barton. It's a Category 3, but they think it could get bigger."

Josh studied the map, which kept repeating satellite images of the hurricane's path. "Is it headed our way?"

"We should be all right. They think it is headed for northern Mexico."

Josh thanked the man and continued on for his weekly trip to the temple, but all through the endowment session he felt uncomfortable. Finally in the Celestial Room, he prayed, "I can't get that hurricane out of my mind. Is it headed to Guatemala?"

The unmistakable impression came. "*Yes.*"

Josh wasn't sure what to do next. Finally he prayed, "Heavenly Father, tell me what to do."

"*Gather the people here.*"

Josh quickly returned to the mission home and called Church headquarters in Salt Lake to share the prompting with Elder Smith. The apostle conferred with the First Presidency and called Josh back a half hour later to approve his plan to gather the people. Josh then sent out calls for all of the mission's stake presidents to meet together at the temple that evening.

When the stake presidents were settled into the temple chapel, Josh called upon one of them to open the meeting with a prayer, and then he shared with them the impression he had received concerning the hurricane earlier in the day.

 One of the stake presidents then asked, "You want everyone to gather here on the temple grounds? Wouldn't it be easier to just meet at our stake centers?"

Josh shook his head. "I feel the Lord wants the Saints gathered here. The storm is gathering strength and could be devastating."

"I don't know how many of the members would come," another president said.

"Well, maybe this is a test of faith as much as anything," Josh responded. "At the very least, it will be a good test of our preparedness, but I feel it is the real thing."

"Then when should the people gather?" the president asked.

"I would begin by having the home teachers begin to spread the word all day tomorrow, and then announce it in your sacrament meetings," Josh said. "It looks like we have a few days before the hurricane will reach us, but I would like each of you here by Sunday night. We'll assign each stake an area of the temple grounds. Then you can organize your area by wards and we'll be able to account for those who have arrived."

"What should the people bring?" another president asked.

"Food and shelter, first of all," Josh said. "I would hope the temple's water supply will hold up, but we will begin filling containers here immediately and transporting them to each stake's area."

After a few more questions, Josh closed the meeting by offering a simple prayer. "Heavenly Father, we thank thee for these righteous men. Please guide us in this effort to protect thy humble Saints. Touch their hearts to follow the counsel of their leaders."

Josh and Kim spent the following morning helping rope off areas of the temple grounds for each of the stakes. It was a beautiful sunny spring day, and a major hurricane seemed unlikely. "Do you think the people will come?" Kim asked.

"They'll come," Josh said.

Sure enough, by that evening people began arriving at the temple grounds. Most carried some food items, and others pulled carts that contained tents and tarps. The members were directed to their stake areas, and Josh noticed that as they got settled, they all subconsciously pointed their tents toward the temple. It brought a lump to Josh's throat. "They are just like King Benjamin's people," he said to himself.

As more and more people gathered, it almost became a festive atmosphere as old friends greeted each other. That night they even gathered in front of the temple, playing musical instruments and dancing together. Kim smiled at Josh. "I think our straight-laced Saints in Utah might frown at this," she said, "but I think it is wonderful."

"I do, too."

As Josh checked the weather reports that night, Hurricane Barton had shifted south from earlier projections. The forecast now was that it would indeed hit Guatemala. Even worse, it had gained strength to a Category 4 storm and had picked up speed. It could hit the temple grounds as soon as Tuesday.

The following day was not a typical Sabbath day in Quetzaltenango. After the announcements were made in the sacrament meetings, the ward buildings were locked up and the majority of the Saints began their journey to the temple.

The stake presidents and bishops were happy to report that essentially every faithful family in the area had chosen to gather at the temple. Now the problem was fitting everyone inside the temple grounds. However, by Monday afternoon everyone was situated, which was a miracle in itself. At about the same time, clouds began to be visible in the eastern sky, and a slight breeze passed through the temple grounds.

The stake presidents met outside the temple, and Tad showed them on a laptop computer the progress of the storm. The hurricane's outer edge had reached Guatemala's eastern coast. Hurricane Barton was now a Category 5 storm with winds approaching 160 miles per hour, one of the strongest storms on record. They were able to watch news footage of the villages on the coastline, and they were being severely ravaged. The stake presidents looked at each other with grim determination, offered another prayer asking for protection, and then they went to their respective stakes to prepare them for what was coming.

Josh and Kim stayed inside the temple with members of the temple presidency. It was a gut-wrenching decision for Josh not to let anyone else in the temple, but it wasn't a time to play favorites. "Were the people really better off here than in their homes or the church buildings?" he asked himself. But the calm assurance of the Spirit confirmed his actions.

At around midnight, the wind began to whistle through the makeshift city, and rain started to fall. The storm's intensity increased throughout the night, and when morning came, no one could really tell, because it was so dark and foreboding.

At around 11 a.m. the hurricane hit with full force, and the entire area was pounded by wind and heavy rain. Some windows in the upper portion of the temple shattered, and soon the winds could be felt swirling inside the building. Josh and Kim huddled together under a blanket in a small meeting room, praying for the Saints outside. The minutes stretched into hours as the wind continually howled, mixed with occasional crashes and other sounds of destruction.

By 3 p.m. there was a noticeable decrease in the winds, and while it was still quite gloomy, there was enough light to begin surveying the damage. Josh and Kim exited the temple as soon as they felt it was safe, and they were dismayed as they looked at the neighborhood surrounding the temple grounds. Nearly all of the buildings were missing their roofs, and many were completely destroyed. The rainfall amounts had been catastrophic, and small rivers ran through the streets. Josh looked at the nearby hillsides and could see several mudslides that had happened overnight.

They hurried onto the temple grounds to check on the members. Everyone and everything were completely drenched, and as the Church members emerged from their tents, there were many reports of injuries. Several people had been injured by flying debris, but no one on the temple grounds had been killed. The Saints considered this to be a great blessing from the Lord.

Josh and Kim spent the next hour helping transport the most severely injured people to the temple, where they could recover more comfortably. Kim helped organize the lobby of the temple into a makeshift hospital, and several members who were doctors or nurses came to the temple to assist the injured Saints.

Meanwhile, Josh and other Church leaders gave each of the wounded members a priesthood blessing, and then the leaders went among the Saints in pairs to give blessings as needed. Despite the destruction that surrounded them, there was a sense of peace and hope among the Saints. Over and over the members told Josh, "The Lord was with us."

As the sun began to set on that difficult day, Josh rejoined Kim in front of the temple. They looked out across the temple grounds at the thousands of faithful Saints working together to straighten their makeshift tents and shelters.

Josh took his wife in his arms, and kissed her forehead. "Thank you for being so faithful," he told her. "If we had just gone inactive in the Church, we could be living in a nice house in the United States and not have to worry about this."

Kim gave him a little jab in the ribs. "Don't even talk that way. I am so grateful to be here. We are living among some of the Lord's most chosen people, and I wouldn't want to be anywhere else."

Just then a ward group nearby began singing a hymn. Soon the unmistakable sound of "Come, Come Ye Saints" sung in Spanish began to spread throughout all of the stakes on the temple grounds. Josh couldn't stop tears from coming to his eyes.

"Yes," he said. "All is well. All is well."

CHAPTER 9

That same week at the end of April, Tad rushed home from work, ate dinner without hardly speaking to Emma and the kids, then headed out the door to meet his friends and attend yet another Gladiatorzz game.

When he returned four hours later, Emma was waiting on the couch for him. She had put the kids to bed nearly two hours before and had spent the rest of the evening pondering what was happening to her marriage.

"With everything that is going on in the world, how come you're still so devoted to that team?" Emma asked. "I'm starting to wonder if they rank higher in your life than I do."

"That's a cheap shot," Tad responded. "You know it is just a way for me to relax."

Emma glared at him. "I don't think so. I think it is a way to hide from your family. You rarely do anything with the boys anymore."

"Hey, I've told you I'd love to take David to the games, but you won't let me."

Emma threw her hands in the air. "I don't understand you. It seems like a burden lately to even get you to go to Church. What happened to the testimony-bearing, faithful man I married?"

"I don't know what you are getting so upset about! We pay our tithing, I go to Elders Quorum—"

"What if I asked you to go to the temple with me on Saturday instead of going to the next Gladiatorzz game?"

Tad hesitated. "Could we go in the morning so I could make it back to the game in time?"

Emma started crying. "I give up."

"What?" Tad said in frustration. "Can't we do both?"

Emma just shook her head and stormed out of the apartment. He watched her walk into the darkness, silently kicking himself for not going after her, especially with the recent rise in violence in their neighborhood since the latest earthquake.

Tad sat down on the couch and punched a cushion. If only Emma knew the inner turmoil he was going through! Didn't Emma realize he only wanted what was best for her and the kids?

Then he looked at the tiny, almost undetectable mark on the back of his right hand where a chip had been implanted. His choice had already been made.

⚜ ⚜ ⚜

When Emma finally returned to the apartment an hour later, she found Tad sitting on the couch. He jumped up and took her hand. "I'm so sorry," he said. "I've been very selfish. I know I need to be a better father and husband."

Emma was silent, but allowed him to hug her. Finally she said, "Do you love us enough to give up the Gladiatorzz?"

"What do you mean?" he asked.

"Will you sell your season tickets?" Emma asked.

"I suppose so. Do I have any options?"

Emma stepped back and looked him in the eyes. "Well, if you don't sell them, I will wonder where we stand in your life."

Tad nodded. "I'll get rid of them, if it's that important."

"Believe me, it is."

"I'll put them up for sale on eBay tomorrow."

⚜ ⚜ ⚜

The next morning they had a pleasant breakfast together, and Tad gave Emma a nice kiss as he departed for work. She sent the kids off to school and then had a productive morning taking care of the housework. She felt better about their marriage than she had in quite a while.

At around noon, she heard the postman put their mail in the box. She retrieved it and sorted through a pile of credit card offers and bills. At the bottom of the pile was a yellow envelope addressed to Tad. The return address was from a federal office in Salt Lake City.

Emma curiously opened it and found a $2,000 check. Along the bottom-left corner of the check it read in bold letters, "Chip distribution # TN8113104."

"This must be a mistake," Emma said to herself. She noticed there was also a website listed on the check, and she logged in. The site asked for a pin number, and Emma entered in the number at the bottom of the check. When she did, all of Tad's personal information flashed on the screen. According to the website, Tad supposedly received the chip about two weeks earlier.

Emma was so stunned she literally couldn't move for a moment. Could this be true? She slumped off the chair and felt like she was going to throw up. Then her anger overcame her dismay. She grabbed the phone and called Tad at work.

She first casually asked how his day was going. He was in a good mood, and told her he was glad they had patched up their differences.

Then she dropped the bomb on him. "By the way, when were you going to tell me you had received the chip?"

"Uh, what?" Tad said slowly.

"You know, the chip you have in your hand?"

"Emma, I would never get the chip!"

"Then how do you explain the $2,000 check we just received in the mail?"

"There must be a mistake," Tad said hastily.

"Then the number TN8113104 means nothing to you?"

Tad didn't respond for nearly twenty seconds, sweat breaking out on his forehead. *She knew!*

"Look, I did it for our family," Tad finally said. "They were going to fire me if I didn't get it. That check was supposed to come to my office, not to our home."

"At least you have finally told the truth." Emma hung up the phone and broke down in sobs. Tad called back, but Emma unplugged the phone from the wall and turned off her cell phone. What more could he have to say?

After a few minutes, Emma regained her composure and called her father Mark. When he answered, she said, "Dad, I'm sorry to bother you, but could the kids and I come stay with you for a few days while Tad and I work out a few things?"

"Are you okay?" Mark asked her.

"I don't know. We just need a little time apart," Emma said. "Could you come pick us up? I might need you to load up a few items, too."

"This sounds pretty serious," Mark said.

Emma sighed. "It is. Tad got the chip without telling me."

"Whoa. All right. I'll see if Doug can help us out. I should be able to get there by the time your kids get home from school. Will that work?"

"That will be great. I love you."

"I love you, too," Mark said. "Everything will work out."

After Emma wouldn't answer his calls, Tad sat and stewed in his office for the next hour, trying to sort out the mess his life had suddenly become. On one hand he wanted to rush home, but on the other hand, he really didn't want to. It was a strange feeling. He felt guilty, but he also felt liberated somehow.

Finally at 3 p.m. he caught the TRAX train and headed home. As Tad approached the apartment, he was surprised to see Mark's truck backed up to the front door. It was filled with the kids' beds and drawers.

"Hey, isn't this a little quick?" he said as Mark came out of the door with Leah's stuffed animals.

Mark put the dolls in the truck, then turned to his son-in-law. "Tad, for the past two hours I've pictured myself hitting you in the face. Do you want that to happen?"

Tad took a step backward. "Of course not."

"Then you better stay out of the way."

Doug soon came out of the apartment with an armful of clothes, and could only give Tad a sad shake of the head.

At that moment, Emma brought the kids out to the minivan. She forced a smile on her face and said, "Give your dad a hug, kids. We're going on a little vacation to grandpa and grandma's house."

David looked concerned. He had overheard some of his parents' late-night conversations, and he was old enough to know his parents were having problems. He gave Tad a hug and whispered, "You're not getting divorced, are you?"

Tad held his son tight. "No, don't worry. Things are going to be fine. Take care of your mom until we're together again."

Then he hugged the other kids, and turned to Emma. She kept her distance. She said, "I love you, but you've got to put your family first. Call me in a couple of days."

"I'm sorry, Emma. Please don't go."

"I hope you're sorry, but I need a break," she said.

She turned away and got in the minivan. Within a minute they were driving away. Emma didn't speak as they drove to Springville. Her world felt shattered. She had been praying about Tad, and she knew something just wasn't right. There had always been a light in his eyes from the day she met him, but over the past few weeks that light had dimmed.

She had even checked the hard drive of their home computer while he was at work, worried Tad may have been into pornography or visiting improper chat rooms, but she didn't find anything out of the ordinary. She never would have guessed he would get the chip, though.

"This isn't really happening," Tad told himself as he watched the truck and minivan disappear down the road. He went into the apartment and taped to their bedroom door was the $2,000 check. Emma had written on a Post-It note: "*Don't forget to deposit this.*" It felt like a slap in the face.

Tad had a horrible night's sleep, feeling dark inside. He

considered using his priesthood to cast out the evil feeling in the apartment, but he didn't feel worthy.

He still felt anxious to talk to Emma, and he called her from work the next day. He was disappointed that she didn't seem to miss him as much as he had hoped.

"We're doing fine," Emma said. "I really don't plan on going back to that apartment."

Tad was flustered. "So are we separating? What do you expect from me?"

"First of all, I expect you to return that check and get the chip removed. Until that happens, I don't see a lot of options."

"Emma! Don't you see the consequences I would face? I'd lose my job, plus probably get questioned by the government. Besides, I'm right on the brink of getting a great raise. Are you willing to throw that all away?"

After a long pause, Emma said, "Let me put it this way. I'm willing to trust in the Lord and put our lives in his hands, but it doesn't sound like you are."

"You need to realize I did this for you, not for me," Tad said. "You deserve a house of your own, and I want to buy you one. The kids deserve to have their own backyard to play in. We're so close to getting that! But it won't ever happen if I remove the chip. Just come back to the apartment, and we'll work things out."

Emma sighed. "No, Tad. I never want to go back to that neighborhood. I feel so much more peaceful already."

"Well, why don't you start looking for a house down there?" Tad asked, suddenly feeling hopeful. "I'll stay here and keep things afloat for now. That way we'll have both bases covered. Then once you find a house, I'll make the commute. It will be worth it for our family."

"You didn't listen to me," Emma said, getting increasingly irritated. "Call me back when you get rid of the chip."

"Don't give up yet, Emma," Tad said, oblivious to his wife's concerns. "We'll work this out."

CHAPTER 10

Emma attended church on the first Sunday in May with her parents at Springville's historic meetinghouse located on the corner of 300 East and Center Street. It was a beautiful day, and the sunlight shone through the windows, brightening the chapel.

She had loved attending there when she was growing up, and she had always enjoyed looking at the four unique murals on the chapel's north wall. The murals were the actual plaster molds of the bronze plaques that were placed on the four sides of the monument atop the Hill Cumorah, and each mural depicted a key moment from the restoration of the gospel.

The church had been built at the same time the monument was completed, and rather than destroy the molds, they had been incorporated into the chapel's design.

Emma once again studied those murals as she waited for the meeting to begin, unaware this would be an unforgettable day in Church history that would affect millions of members.

She did notice, however, that the bishopric seemed on edge. They usually mingled with the congregation for a few minutes before the start of sacrament meeting, and Bishop Cluff always made a point to shake her hand whenever she visited. But today the bishopric came in together and went straight to their seats on the stand. The bishop looked nervous and even a little pale.

As a few latecomers settled into their seats, the opening hymn was sung, followed by a short prayer. Then Bishop Cluff moved to the pulpit. He shuffled his notes, then held a paper in front of him. He said, "We have a received a letter from our Area Presidency that

I have been asked to read. I will do so at this time. It says:

"To the LDS Church members in the Utah South Area:

"In recent General Conference addresses and in several Ensign magazine articles, the First Presidency and the Quorum of the Twelve Apostles have given repeated warnings to both the nation and to the members of the Church. They have spoken of the need for spiritual and temporal preparedness in anticipation of upcoming events that will transpire if the commandments of God are ignored. These prophetic warnings have largely gone unheeded, and the Lord will soon fulfill his promises as outlined in the Doctrine and Covenants.

"Therefore, under the direction of the First Presidency, we issue an invitation of gathering to you. The Church has prepared gathering places along the Wasatch Front where members of the Church can be shielded from any turmoil that may soon come upon our nation. Your local leaders have been given specific instructions on where your particular stake has been assigned to gather.

"Sincerely,

"The Utah South Area Presidency"

Bishop Cluff looked up from the letter and said, "We have been assigned to gather with the other wards in our stake. Our assigned gathering place is the Jolley's Ranch campground in Hobble Creek Canyon."

Emma took a glance at Doug, who didn't seem at all surprised by this announcement.

The bishop added, "As the letter says, the gathering is to begin now. We have made copies of the letter for every family in the ward, and we ask that every home teaching companionship makes sure your assigned families receive a copy if they aren't in attendance today."

The congregation had been listening intently, but now the members exploded into a flurry of questions. The bishop motioned for silence, and then continued, "There will be a semi-trailer brought to the Church this afternoon. All families who choose to gather with the stake should bring their food storage to the trailer.

There will be buses leaving for the camp this evening at 5 p.m. Attached to the letter is a checklist of other acceptable items, such as clothing, that can be brought to the camp in suitcases. These will be loaded onto the buses. Certain pets may be allowed, such as a household cat or dog, but I must approve any pets that are brought to the camp."

Bishop Cluff then paused and grimaced a little, realizing the pet issue would probably be his most difficult chore of the day. Then a wave of emotion crossed his face. "As your bishop, I emphasize that this gathering is strictly voluntary, but I encourage you to follow our leaders. My family and I will be on a bus this afternoon, along with my counselors and their families. I hope you will be, too."

The bishop paused again to gather his emotions. "We have been told to have you return to your homes at this time. This announcement is being made in wards all along the Wasatch Front and also in surrounding states. We know this will be a difficult decision, but we know that if you ask the Lord in humility, you will receive an answer about whether this is the right decision for you. I close this meeting in the name of Jesus Christ, Amen."

Bishop Cluff stepped away from the pulpit, and the congregation sat in stunned silence. Someone called out, "This is some sort of a joke, right?"

But the bishopric showed no sign of humor, and they left the stand and exited the chapel. Conversations erupted all over the chapel, and there was genuine disharmony among some families. Leah started crying.

Doug put his arm around Emma's shoulder. "This isn't the best atmosphere to make plans. Let's go back to Dad's house and talk about it."

Once the Dalton family was gathered in the living room, Mark stood before them and asked if they would follow the invitation of the First Presidency and go to the Jolley's Ranch camp.

"Of course," David said.

Mark smiled at him. "That's the right attitude. Is there anyone who doesn't want to go?"

"I want to go, but what about my dad?" Charles asked. "Is he going to be with us?"

There was an uncomfortable silence, then Emma said, "I'll call him and see if he wants to come."

Mark nodded. "Very well. Okay, let's begin gathering our food storage out of the cellar and take it to the trailer at the Church."

As everyone began pitching in, Doug took Emma aside. "The bishop didn't mention it, but once we are all settled at the camp, we are going to carefully guard the camp entrance. It is to protect us from people trying to overrun our camp looking for food when things get bad. So if Tad doesn't join us today, he probably won't be able to later. Maybe you should tell him that when you call him."

Emma frowned. "I doubt that will matter to him, because I'm pretty sure he won't come."

"I don't think he will, either, but that way you'll at least have made the effort."

Emma called the apartment, and Tad answered after eight rings.

"Did I wake you?" Emma asked.

"Actually, yeah. I didn't really feel like going to Church and having to explain that my wife had left me."

"Well, maybe you should have gone." She then told him about the letter the bishop had read and her intention to go to the Jolley's Ranch campground with her family.

Tad couldn't believe what he was hearing. "This has to just be a test of some sort," he said. "The economy is booming and there is no threat of an attack. I can't believe how paranoid the Church leaders are, and your family believes every word they say."

Emma was saddened by his response. "I'm going to the camp," she told him. "I know it is the right thing to do."

"What are the kids going to do? They can come live with me if they want."

"They said they will follow the prophet," Emma said.

"It's not that simple! Are you just sheep following a bunch of old men around?"

Tad's words really hurt her. Not because he essentially called her a blind follower, but because it showed how far he had slipped.

"You know we aren't sheep. We are following the Lord's prophet," Emma said. "Tad, it really *is* that simple."

Tad finally lost his cool. "I'm not the one tearing our family apart. You're the one who is selfishly taking my children away!"

Tad slammed down the phone, disgusted at his wife. He got dressed and walked over to their ward building. A large truck was being loaded with food and supplies. A ward member noticed him and waved. Tad waved back, but he was certainly not in a mood to answer any questions.

He hurried back to the apartment and turned on the TV. He flipped through the local stations and was surprised that there wasn't any mention on the news of the Church's announcement. He figured no one had tipped off the media yet.

For a moment he felt nervous and wondered if he could be wrong. Then he shook his head. These mountain camps must only be a mock-disaster drill the Church was conducting. Even when Doug had talked to them about the Church's preparations, it had sounded outlandish. It seemed to him that if the Saints were going to gather in the mountains, it would be in a time of emergency, not when everything was going so well.

Emma and the kids spent the afternoon helping her parents haul their large stash of food storage to the trailer in the church parking lot. She wished she had more of her own food storage to contribute, but under the circumstances, it was understandable.

The checklist with the letter encouraged each member to bring clothing for summer and winter weather, and they sorted through their clothing and packed them in suitcases. Emma was glad she had brought all of the kids' clothing from the Sandy apartment. There was a sense of excitement in the air, but Emma still felt nervous, particularly about Tad.

"Do you think I'll see my husband again?" she asked Doug.

"I'm afraid it will depend on what Tad chooses to do," Doug said. "As I've attended these preparedness meetings over the past few months, several times the leaders mentioned this event would divide families. But I always thought Tad would be right there by my side. I'm praying he'll realize he's on the wrong side of the line before it's too late."

As 5 p.m. approached, a few more families joined the group in the Church parking lot, but there were even more members of the Church standing nearby trying to talk them out of going to the camp.

One of the Doug's neighbors, a young guy named Barry Newton, came up to him. Doug had been Barry's home teacher for several months, but he could never get him to come to Church. "Hey Doug, it looks like you're heading out with the group," Barry said. "Does this mean I can have your snowblower?"

Doug looked at his neighbor. "Once we are gone, you can have whatever you want. It's not going to matter soon anyway."

Barry raised his eyebrows. "What do you mean?"

Doug just shook his head. "I just wish you would join us."

"You've always been a little different, Doug. Can't you see this is all a false alarm?"

"Well, I'm afraid it isn't, but you've been a good neighbor." Then Doug smiled. "Well, Barry, it looks like I finally got you to Church—or at least to the parking lot."

Barry laughed, and the men shook hands. Similar exchanges took place among other neighbors, but people had already decided whether they were going to follow the words of the prophet. No one was switching sides at this point.

At 5 p.m. two buses pulled into the parking lot, and the bishop called together the ward members who were going to the camp. Each bus would hold 50 people, and sadly, everyone from their ward who had decided to follow the prophet fit on one bus. The bishop told the other bus driver they wouldn't need him, so the driver departed to see if he would be needed at the stake center.

Emma helped her children onto the bus, and they were joined

by Doug, Becky, and their two little ones. Emma's parents had already gone up to the camp in their roles as missionaries to make sure everything was ready for the group's arrival.

There was a sense of finality as the bus door closed. Their neighbors were still in the parking lot, and they waved good-bye as the bus pulled onto Center Street and headed east. Some of the neighbors had been sitting in church with them that morning, and now they were laughing and pointing at them.

"They're mocking us," David said, a little upset.

"That's true," Emma said, putting her hand on his leg. "But that's all right. It seems the Lord's people always get mocked for doing the right thing. So take it as a compliment."

The bus traveled up Center Street then turned right onto 1300 East, heading for Hobble Creek Canyon. They passed Child Park, where a few families were enjoying their Sunday afternoon by playing on the playground and kicking a soccer ball around. It seemed as if they didn't have a care in the world.

The buses from the other seven wards in the stake arrived at the camp. Some of the wards had required two or three buses, so the turnout from some wards had been higher. All together only 600 members of the stake had come to the camp from a stake of 4,000 people.

Each Springville stake was assigned to a different area of Church-owned property throughout Hobble Creek Canyon, while the Saints from the Mapleton stakes were gathering in Maple Canyon. This pattern was being followed up and down the Wasatch Front, with stakes gathering on Church-owned property in the canyon closest to their homes.

After all the buses were unloaded and the semi-trailer emptied of its food storage, the vehicles went back down the canyon, leaving the group without motorized vehicles except for a few four-wheelers that the work missionaries already had at the camp. As the last bus drove away, priesthood leaders began to pull tents out of the storage sheds and organize themselves according to wards.

People were working hard and cooperating well, but a feeling of gloom settled on the camp as it began to sink in to everyone that this was for real, and that they weren't going back. They had left their homes, jobs, cars, and everything else. They believed they were following the words of the prophet, but that didn't make it any easier. Just that morning they had gone to church expecting to have a normal Sunday, and now they were suddenly camping out for an undetermined amount of time. The fact they had packed winter clothes meant it could be at least several months.

Doug had noticed the change in everyone's attitude and took their stake president aside. "President Johnson, we need to hold a sacrament meeting," Doug told him. "It will help everyone get on the same page and boost their spirits."

President Johnson agreed. "After the sacrament, would you say a few words, since you've done such a great job coordinating the preparation of this camp?"

"I would love to," Doug said.

They quickly spread the word that everyone should stop what they were doing and gather under the main pavilion for a meeting. Once everyone was gathered around under the pavilion, President Johnson praised them for following the prophet. He bore his testimony that they had made the right choice.

He said, "Even the strongest among us have struggled with this decision. Look around. Where are our young families, and where are our older members? Some might say that the Lord asks too much of us, but I don't think so."

President Johnson then invited the stake high council to come forward. Nine men joined him. He continued, "As you can see, three members of our stake high council have chosen not to join us. That is disappointing, but we will move forward. We also have fewer people here than we usually have at a stake conference. Why aren't those people here? There are many reasons, but mostly because they have chosen the things of the world. The time has come for the Latter-day Saints to become a Zion people. This is the first step.

The Lord isn't going to force anyone to be part of Zion. He has invited us. I know we might go through a period of difficulties, but if we work together, we can avoid serious problems. Thankfully all of our bishops are here, and we will prepare ourselves to be worthy of the Lord's blessings."

President Johnson asked all members of the Aaronic Priesthood to come forward. "This is a little unusual, since we don't have sacrament trays unpacked yet, but we have some bread here, and some cups of water. We dismissed our meetings this morning before we could partake of the sacrament, and I feel it is important that we do so tonight. We'll bless the sacrament and then have each Aaronic Priesthood holder make sure his family and ward members receive the bread and water."

President Johnson asked one of the priests to offer the sacramental prayer on the bread, and then the other young men distributed it. David was one of them, and he carried pieces of bread to his family and then took a piece himself.

A reverent spirit descended on the group, and David in particular felt very emotional and had to wipe his eyes. He couldn't help thinking of his father, the man who had ordained him a priest just a couple of months earlier. He still couldn't really grasp that Tad had chosen to separate himself from his family.

After the cups of water were passed, the priesthood holders returned to their seats. Then Doug stood and addressed the group. "My name is Doug Dalton, and since I am the Stake Preparedness Coordinator, President Johnson asked me to say a few words to close our meeting," he said. "Many of you don't know me, and you probably didn't even know this calling existed, but I have helped organize this camp for several months. I know the preparations that were made here were inspired by the Lord. He knew we would need a place of protection from the judgments that are coming to our nation."

He paused to look around the group, and he noticed some glum looks. He continued, "But I don't want to dwell on the negative aspects. This really is an important day in the history of the Church, and I'm grateful to be a part of it. I hope you are, too. I commend you for having the faith to leave your homes and most of your earthly possessions. I know if we keep the commandments, we will prosper and earn an eternal reward far greater than the things we have left behind."

Doug paused to look at the faithful Saints that surrounded him, and he was pleased to see most of them seemed happy to be there, rather than moping about their situation. He wanted the younger children to understand the importance of the day, so he aimed the next part of his message at them.

"You may have noticed some of our neighbors making fun of us as we left," Doug said. "Can you think of anywhere in the scriptures where people have been mocked for following the Lord?"

Emma's daughter Leah raised her hand. "The people in the big building laughed at Nephi when he was holding onto the Iron Rod."

That's right," Doug said. "And what happened to those people in the building who were making fun of the others?"

Charles answered, "The building fell and the people were destroyed because they wouldn't do what was right."

"Very good," Doug said. "There are a lot of instances in the scriptures of the Lord's followers being teased. This even has happened a lot in Church history. But there is one story in particular that applies to what we have done today. It involves a big boat."

Several hands shot up, and a few called out, "Noah's ark!"

"Yes, Noah was told to build a ship and be prepared for the flood. His neighbors made fun of him, but he followed the Lord and he and his family members were saved. By choosing to come to this camp, we are figuratively stepping into Noah's ark. He built his ark before there were any rain clouds in the sky. It didn't seem like there was any real danger until Noah and his family were safely in the ark. Do you see the similarity to what we have done today?"

Several people in the group nodded in understanding. Doug concluded, "We have done what the Lord's prophet has asked us to do. People may laugh at us and say we are stupid for leaving our homes, but I testify to you that the Lord has told us to stand in holy places, and I promise that where you are right now is a holy place. This is the *right* place for you to be. I say this in the name of Jesus Christ, Amen."

At that moment the Spirit of the Lord descended on the camp, and a sense of happiness filled the members' hearts. Doug gave a big smile, then said, "Okay, bishops, let's finish getting those tents set up!"

CHAPTER 11

In Guatemala, the miracle of the Saints' gathering before the hurricane hit became more evident as the days went on. The women and children remained on the temple grounds as the men returned to their homes to assess the damage. They all universally reported the same thing. Their homes had either been severely damaged or were simply gone, and many of their neighbors had been killed.

There were so many people killed throughout Quetzaltenango that their bodies were wrapped in sheets and taken to public parks. But the heat and humidity that followed the storm was causing rapid decay of the bodies, and city officials were soon forced to dig mass graves that were filled with thousands of bodies.

Quetzaltenango would never be the same. The city had been devastated by the hurricane, and the citizens began to call it "The City of Death."

Within days, a good portion of the non-LDS citizens had already left the area. Many citizens had struggled to find work and housing even before the hurricane, and now that the city was a disaster area, they desperately wanted to try somewhere else. There wasn't any gasoline available for cars or buses, but that didn't stop them. The roads out of Quetzaltenango were clogged day and night as people headed on foot toward either to Guatemala City or Mexico, hoping to start a better life.

Meanwhile, the Saints began repairing many of the buildings near the temple site, and an LDS community began to form around the temple. Josh had originally wondered whether he should officially release his missionaries and let them return to their families, but he didn't feel prompted to do so. They were working hard and helping out in so many ways. Josh also sensed that the Lord wanted them to be a part of the upcoming events that Elder Smith had said this group would experience.

Besides, the missionaries were all having a blast. They spent their days working on patching up the temple windows and helping with the work on the surrounding buildings. Despite the disaster, a true spirit of unity could be felt among the missionaries, and Kim admitted she had never felt happier.

One day while Josh was visiting a stake that was living in the far corner of the temple grounds, he was approached by a man who appeared to be in his late 20s. He had toned skin like most other Guatemalans, but Josh couldn't help notice his light brown hair and strikingly blue eyes.

The man took off his work gloves and stuck out his hand. "Elder Brown, it is nice to finally meet you. I have heard many great things about you."

Josh smiled at the man. "I'm glad to meet you, too. What is your name?"

"I'm Brother Mathoni. I grew up in this area, and I thought I'd give you a hand if you need it."

"I appreciate the offer, " Josh said. "Have you been a member of the Church for a while?"

Brother Mathoni nodded. "My family and I were among the first to accept Christ's teachings."

"That's great," Josh said. "Since so many of the members are recent converts, it is nice to meet someone who has a bit of experience in the Church."

Brother Mathoni pointed to a nearby group. "I'm helping this ward get organized, but don't hesitate to find me if you need anything."

"Thank you," Josh said. "I will certainly keep that in mind."

They shook hands again, and Brother Mathoni stared right

into Josh's eyes. It was almost unnerving. As Josh watched Brother Mathoni walk happily away, he said to himself, "There is something definitely unique about that guy."

Three weeks after the hurricane's arrival, very few people remained in Quetzaltenango other than the Saints. On that day, mountains on opposite ends of the valley began to smoke. Small earthquakes were felt, and then Santa Maria, the mountain to the south that towered above the main road to Guatemala City, erupted in a spectacular explosion.

Volcanic ash shot into the sky, but thankfully it drifted away from Quetzaltenango. Josh sent a group of elders to check on the road, and they reported that the canyon was closed off by a thick river of mud and ash.

Three days later, other mountains to the northeast erupted on a smaller scale, putting twenty feet of rubble throughout the bottom of the canyon. The people weren't completely trapped, but no one could get in or out of the valley without taking winding roads through the backcountry, and few people were willing to do that. So the valley was essentially sealed from the outside world.

As the reports came in, Josh felt a bit discouraged. He asked Kim, "Sheesh, can't Mother Nature give us a break?"

But she was more thoughtful. "Maybe it is a way to protect us. I'm sure the Lord's hand is in it."

CHAPTER 12

⚜

Back at the Jolley's Ranch campground, things were going as well as could be expected. Families were getting accustomed to living in their tents and eating meals as a group. The campground itself covered several dozen acres in the bottom of the canyon, and so there was room for everyone. Each ward had set up their tents in assigned parts of the campground, and life proceeded normally.

Of course, as often happens in such situations, a few families had been chronic complainers from the start. One lady complained about having to live in a tent when she had a perfectly good 20-foot-long trailer sitting in her driveway at home.

Another problem was that several teenagers and children were struggling to cope without their cell phones, laptops, iPods and the latest high-tech video games. A few of the kids had smuggled these items onto the bus, and a couple of the teenage girls had been calling their friends down in Springville. This caused a bit of an uproar, and all electronic equipment was confiscated.

President Johnson called an emergency meeting, and explained that at the camp they intended to live in a way that doesn't allow distinctions between the rich and the poor.

"We are all starting fresh," he told the group. "We don't care if you made a million dollars a year or if you were on welfare. The important thing is that we are united in our purpose to become more Christlike. That is why we all live in tents. It would create an imbalance if some people had their trailers and RVs, while others lived in pup tents. The electronic items create the same divisions."

One of the fathers of the "cell phone girls" raised his hand.

"Well, we came here voluntarily," the man said. "Does that mean we can leave whenever we want?"

President Johnson nodded, but he pointed to the fence that surrounded the campground. "Just be aware, though, that once you leave you won't be welcomed back."

The cell-phone daughter said, "Good! It's not like I'd ever want to come back to this stupid place. Just give me my phone back!"

A few other families seemed to agree with the girl, and President Johnson asked, "How many of you would like to leave the camp?"

About ten families raised their hands. President Johnson noted it was the same families that had been causing all the dissension. He said, "You are free to leave. We will gladly return your electronic items, and you can depart whenever you would like."

A lady called out, "So when will the bus be here?"

President Johnson couldn't help smiling. "I'm afraid there aren't any buses scheduled to come to the campground anytime soon. You'll have to walk or hope someone passes by to give you a ride. Don't worry, though. It's only a few miles to the edge of town."

That led to additional grumbling and moaning, but within an hour that group of families had left the camp. The remaining Saints were doing their best to feel sympathetic for the members who had left, because the departed members didn't seem to realize they would face greater challenges back in the valley. But the Saints admittedly felt relieved to have the contention disappear from the camp, and there were plenty of smiles exchanged when the complainers were finally gone.

For Emma, the highlight of the camp so far had been getting to know Doug's wife Becky even better than before. They had always dreamed of living close to each other, and while this wasn't exactly what they had planned, they formed a true sisterly bond.

One morning, Becky was feeling quite sick. She threw up a couple of times, and finally found Emma.

"Can you help me with the chores today?" she asked. "I just

can't seem to keep any food down."

"I would be glad to," Emma said. "Is there anything else I can do for you?"

Becky smiled slyly. "Actually, there is. Can you find me a pregnancy test?"

Emma chuckled as she turned to go to the medical tent. "Lay down on that cot, and I'll be right back."

The camp had a variety of medical supplies, and Emma dug through a supply box until she found what she was looking for. She returned and handed it to Becky, who disappeared for a few minutes before rushing back excitedly into the tent.

"It's official," she told Emma. They hugged each other and then they went to find Doug. They discovered he had actually been searching for them.

"Becky, someone told me you were sick," he said, "so I was going to come give you a blessing if you needed one."

His wife smiled. "I'm feeling a little better now, but maybe you're the one who will need a blessing. We're going to have another baby!"

Doug looked positively shocked. "Really? How?"

They all had a good laugh at his comment, and then they returned to camp to share the good news with everyone else.

By the end of May, the camp at Jolley's Ranch had turned into a small community, equipped with all the items the Saints would need. A large pavilion had been closed in with plywood on all sides and painted white to create an all-purpose meeting room. During the week it served as the dining area, and on Sunday it became the meetinghouse, with each ward having an assigned time for sacrament meeting throughout the day.

The foresight to install a hydraulic generator in Hobble Creek the year before had already paid off. The electricity made everything so much easier at the camp, from preparing meals to holding meetings in the lighted pavilion each night. Another benefit of electrical power was that the stake president could keep in contact with the general authorities through the laptop computer the Church had assigned to him.

Each stake president and general authority throughout the world had been given a laptop computer that could receive transmissions from a satellite. This allowed the leaders to access a Church-owned, encrypted network that provided continuous updates on Church and world situations. Leaders were also able to e-mail Church headquarters or other leaders throughout the world as needed.

To the rest of the world, the Church had seemingly disappeared into the mountains. But in reality, the leaders were in constant contact with each other and preparing for the next phase of the gathering of the Saints. The area presidencies were still fully functioning, and in a real sense, the chain of communication from the prophet down to the stake presidents was more efficient than ever before.

For the time being, however, most Saints at the mountain camps weren't aware of the Church's specific plans. They were encouraged to settle in and build new communities. Large gardens were planted, and some camps even had cows and chickens.

At the Jolley's Ranch camp, each ward was assigned a garden area in a nearby field. The canyon wasn't an ideal place to grow crops, but any type of fresh produce would be welcomed. The stake president announced a friendly competition to see which ward could grow the most carrots, potatoes, tomatoes, and other vegetables by the end of the summer, and the wards eagerly jumped at the chance.

An existing irrigation ditch was widened from Hobble Creek to the garden area, and even the small children took part in the gardening by weeding their ward's portion of the field—with parents carefully watching to make sure the kids only uprooted weeds and not vegetables.

For the most part, the citizens from the valley had left them alone. The camp's northern fence bordered the canyon road, and every once in a while people would drive by and yell things like "Hey losers, get a real job!" But no one at the camp paid them any attention.

One time when Emma and Leah were working in a garden plot that could be seen from the road, a bunch of grungy, wild-haired teenagers drove by in a jeep and shouted, "Look at the hippies." Emma explained to Leah that hippies were people that had long hair and rarely bathed or shaved.

"Then we aren't hippies," Leah said. "They looked more like hippies than we do."

Emma smiled. "That's right. So don't worry about it."

In many ways, everyone felt more productive than they ever had before. Becky, the former elementary school teacher, was named the principal of the camp's school. She organized the children into classes, and Emma was among the teachers who taught the children the gospel straight out of the scriptures. They also taught the children math and history, and school lasted about three hours each day. At first the children didn't want to go to school, but soon it was a favorite part of their day.

While Becky was overseeing the school, Michelle and a few other grandmothers organized a pre-school for the youngest children. Becky's children Justin and Heather really enjoyed their time with their grandma, and Becky welcomed the break.

After the group of "unhappy campers" had left the first week, there weren't a lot of teenagers in the camp, but the ones that had stayed received all kinds of training. There were several gospel scholars in the stake, and they taught the teenagers from the Doctrine and Covenants about the wonderful prophecies that would be fulfilled in their lifetimes. Several Saints had brought Church reference books with them, and one of the tents was transformed into a small library where the members could study. All of these resources helped the youth feel a greater purpose for why they were in the camp, and what awaited them.

Another uplifting part of camp involved the stake patriarch. He worked with the bishops to make appointments with anyone in the camp who had never received a partriarchal blessing, and through those blessings many testimonies were strengthened as the patriarch was able to share with those members the important tasks they would complete in their lives.

The teenagers also received plenty of "temporal" learning as well. The women made sure each of the girls could cook a variety of meals and could sew any kind of clothing. Soon the young women were the ones happily preparing the nightly meal rather than the women, and the food actually tasted better, although the men were smart enough not to say so.

As for the boys, several of the men took turns teaching them important skills ranging from plumbing to laying bricks as they constructed a new building that would serve as a kitchen. Doug also spent a few days teaching them what he had learned as a physical therapist, and it helped them all stay in better health and avoid pulling any muscles as they worked on the projects.

When Emma had packed her belongings to bring to the camp, she had included her clarinet. Now that the camp was functioning well, she asked Doug, "Do you think President Johnson would approve if we turned Friday night into a social night?"

"What do you mean?"

"Well, maybe we could have a dance each Friday," Emma said. "I would like to organize a little band. I've got my clarinet, and I know a few other people brought their instruments, too."

Doug pondered the idea. "I don't see why not. When the pioneers were crossing the Plains, they certainly kept up their spirits with square dances and fiddles. I would think we can dance as well as they did!"

President Johnson really liked Emma's suggestion, and she quickly went to work organizing the band. There were a couple of other clarinets in the camp, and four violins. Each of their owners were talented musicians, and they were eager to play again.

They hiked a short distance into a nearby canyon and began practicing songs out of the Church hymnbook. After a couple of hours they sounded great on several hymns.

"Wow, I think we can make this work," Emma told the group. "But we probably need a few really upbeat songs so that everyone isn't slow dancing all the time. Have you heard this one?"

She then played a rousing number that made the group want to get up and dance. "What song is that?" one of the men asked. "It sounds familiar, but I can't quite place it."

Emma laughed. "It's the song the fiddlers play during the 'barn raising' in the movie 'Back to the Future III.' I think it was the band ZZ Top that performed it. You fiddlers should have a blast with that one."

The group soon picked up the tune, and within a half hour the band's version sounded better than the original. They finally took a break, laughing and out of breath.

"Good job! We've got to have a little fun, too," Emma said. "Well, I think we're ready!"

The first dance was the following night, and it was a smashing success. People said they hadn't had so much fun in a long time. President Johnson had such a good time that he declared that they would be holding a short devotional every Monday, Wednesday, and Friday, followed by an hour of dancing before bedtime. He assigned some of the older couples to teach the group traditional dances each week that they had learned as teenagers.

Doug had a funny idea, and he told Emma about it. She raised her eyebrows. "Do you think the stake president is going to be all right with that dance?"

"He won't mind," Doug said with a smile. "The camp will never forget it. Just make sure the band learns the song."

Doug was right about his idea being memorable. Never had a group of Saints ever laughed so hard as Doug taught them the dance moves from Michael Jackson's "Thriller" video. Emma could hardly blow into her clarinet because she kept cracking up.

President Johnson laughed as hard as anyone, but he declared that Doug's dance was permanently banned from the camp. He said, "I'm not banning it because of indecency, but simply to keep us from embarrassing ourselves again."

Doug wholeheartedly agreed.

✣ ✣ ✣

With the Saints safely tucked away in their mountain camps, mainstream society began to unravel. It seemed Satan and his followers had been unleashed in America's cities. The country's morality was already in steep decline, but within weeks the decency standards slipped to unthinkable levels. The idea of "anything goes" became the prevailing attitude.

That summer a movie that was rated NC-17 was shown uncut on a major broadcast network, and pornographic movies became commonplace on basic cable stations. It became clear that the entire American culture was obsessed with sex. Some reports showed that nearly 85 percent of all American men had developed some form of pornography addiction, and sadly, only 10 percent said they felt guilty about it.

The basic concepts of marriage and fidelity were openly mocked. The few practicing Christians who still dared to stand up for decency were often brutally beaten, and religious buildings across the nation were burned or covered with graffiti.

One valiant Baptist minister led a small rally on the steps of the Lincoln Memorial in the nation's capital, trying to warn Congress that the Lord would not always stay His hand.

The preacher shouted, "We are fast approaching the days of Sodom and Gomorrah. How much longer can we expect God to spare us? We are ignoring His teachings. Our Congress no longer follows the Constitution, and our Supreme Court is making decisions that mock heaven itself. I declare that this nation has turned its back on God, and we deserve whatever Biblical judgments await us!"

The crowd booed the minister's words. As policemen began

to close in on him, he raised his voice even higher. "The many recent earthquakes across the land are a sign from God, as if the earth itself is disgusted with its inhabitants. Mount Vesuvius once covered the sins of Pompeii with fire and brimstone. Can we expect anything less?"

At that point the preacher was knocked to the ground by two policemen, who kicked him in the head. Other bystanders kicked the minister in the ribs and spit on him before the policemen finally dragged him away to a van where they permanently put a stop to his preaching.

The newspaper the next morning had a small headline buried deep in the Metro Section that read, "Baptist minister dies while resisting arrest."

Unfortunately for America, that minister had been right. With such wickedness spreading across the land, the Lord wouldn't stay His hand much longer.

CHAPTER 13

⸎

It was now June, and Tad still hadn't been to Springville since the fateful day a month earlier when Emma had left with the kids. He knew they were now at the Jolley's Ranch campground, but he just couldn't convince himself to drive up the canyon. He had heard that all of the mountain camps were surrounded by fences and he didn't want to have to explain himself to anyone at the gate. Besides, he had no intention of staying at the camp, and he doubted they had a visitor's pass.

Plus, the guilt of still having the chip in his hand deterred him from wanting to see his family. He loved them dearly, but he couldn't bear to see their pained expressions. He was sure his sons had lost their respect for him.

The more practical reason he hadn't gone to Springville was Emma had taken the minivan. He could have taken the TRAX train there, but then he would have to walk several blocks through downtown Springville, and the streets there weren't as safe as they had been before the Saints left town.

Finally he decided to cash his $2,000 "chip check" and use the money as a down-payment on a little 2009 Porsche sports car. The car was a few years old, but it was really fun to drive and he had negotiated a good deal on it.

That evening Tad zoomed down to Springville, telling himself it was his duty to make sure the Daltons' house was kept in good shape and hadn't been vandalized. As he pulled in front of the house, he saw their minivan parked in the driveway with a note taped to the windshield. He grabbed the note and saw it was in

Emma's handwriting. It read, "*Tad, you can take the van. We won't be using it anymore.*"

Tad crumpled up the note. "You'll need the van when you get back," he said as he glanced at his shiny silver Porsche. "Besides, the van has been replaced."

Tad decided to attend his West Jordan ward the following Sunday, more out of boredom than anything, but he was curious to see how the remaining members were going to adapt without any leaders. His neighbor had told him the whole bishopric and all the ward leaders had gone to their stake's assigned camp in Little Cottonwood Canyon.

Tad entered the chapel and settled into a pew. There were about 40 people in attendance. He glanced up at the stand and was stunned to see a man named Larry Campbell sitting in the bishop's seat.

"Now I *know* I'm not living right," Tad said to himself.

Larry had once been a prominent Salt Lake attorney, but he was sent to prison for several months for fraud. He lost all of his assets, including his big mansion in east Salt Lake. While he was in prison, he had been hit in the head with a pipe and became somewhat of a religious zealot who sometimes called himself "Sherem" after a person in the Book of Mormon. He was best known for writing strange letters to the *Deseret News*, asking to have a debate with the prophet.

Larry had been released from prison three months earlier and was living in a halfway house in their ward boundaries. Now with the bishopric gone, he seemed eager to fill the vacancy.

Larry stood up and went to the pulpit. "Brothers and sisters, the Spirit has called me to be the new bishop of our ward."

Everyone looked around at each other. Never had there been a more unlikely bishop. Larry then pointed at Tad and said, "Brother North, the Spirit has moved me to call you as my first counselor. Please join me on the stand."

Tad may have been going through a spiritual crisis, but he was certain that the Lord had *not* called him to be Larry Campbell's counselor. Tad called out, "No thanks, Larry. I think I'm going to find another ward."

Larry glared at him. "Brother North, if you reject this calling, you will be cursed by the Lord!"

Tad laughed out loud. Is this what his spiritual life had become? "Larry, I'm not sure things could get much worse for me, but I appreciate the warning," he said. "I wish you the best as bishop."

Tad walked out of the chapel and never returned. Within a week, he heard that Larry was back in prison for a parole violation, and soon the ward meetinghouse was empty each Sunday.

Tad actually had a lot more to worry about besides Larry Campbell's supposed curse as the summer progressed. The national economy took a major downturn. Everyone had rushed to spend their "chip money" on electronic gadgets and vacations, and suppliers rushed to meet demand. They ended up flooding the market with too much merchandise and depressing prices. The temporary economic boom was clearly over, and economists predicted a major recession heading into the second half of the year. Those dire estimates sent a shock through Wall Street and stocks fell rapidly. Millions of investors watched in despair as the value of their 401(k) plans and investment portfolios plummeted.

Throughout the nation, the level of violent crime rose dramatically, particularly in the eastern United States. Urban areas such as northern New Jersey and southern Florida were quickly evolving into battle zones. The National Guard claimed to be monitoring those areas, but they were basically guarding the freeways exits, using tear gas and water cannons to keep people from leaving those areas. The people were essentially being held hostage by their own government, but the politicians didn't want the violence to spread.

Unspeakable horrors were continually taking place among the

citizens in those areas, which the media euphemistically referred to as "red zones." The number of "red zone" murders that summer were never tallied, but they easily totaled in the thousands.

Meanwhile, the federal government had become a huge logjam as the Republican and Democratic leaders in Congress refused to cooperate on major issues. The U.S. president, who just weeks earlier had been a national hero for his chip reimbursement program, was being rightly blamed for propping up everyone's hopes with a short-term solution that hadn't really solved anything.

Publicly, the president acted as if nothing was wrong. He continually asked the American people to "move forward unitedly." He even unveiled his plans to run for re-election, but he knew the nation was in serious trouble. He admitted to his top aides that the country's financial and social quagmire was beyond repair.

As the weeks passed, Tad continued to go to work. Despite the weakening economy and general national unrest, the accounting firm was still doing well. Ken had kept his promises, and Tad was soon promoted with a substantial bonus and raise. He moved out of the Sandy apartment and rented a small one-bedroom apartment in the City Creek Center just across the plaza from his office. He told himself the arrangement would work well for him until Emma and the kids came back down from the mountains.

Now that he didn't have to worry about the lengthy commute he could work late each night, except on the nights of Gladiatorzz games. Despite his promise to Emma, he had never sold the tickets, and he still attended every game with a couple of friends as a way to cope with his lonely, dull life.

Tad had actually enjoyed going to the movies when he was younger, but now there just wasn't anything he wanted to see. There were some new sequels in theaters that summer, but Tad felt the *Pirates of the Caribbean* series had run out of steam after the fifth film, and the *Spider-Man* movies were a joke now without any of the original actors.

However, Tad did have high hopes for *Shrek: The Seventh Son.* The initial reports were it was a funnier film than its predecessor, the way-too-serious *Six Degrees of Shrek.* But after reading a review that said the new movie was "rated R for extreme profanity and animated nudity" he gave up on what Hollywood had to offer.

So with his new raise, a dismal social life and nobody to feed but himself, Tad quickly paid off all of their family debts, including the new car. In fact, he soon had $10,000 sitting in a savings account. Now he was just waiting for Emma to return so they could choose a home together in Springville, just as she had wanted.

Following his job promotion, Tad was given a corner office that had a clear view of the Salt Lake Temple. The rumor around town was that the prophet and some of the Twelve Apostles were living there, and Tad often did see lights shining in the temple's upper windows.

Of course, the temple hadn't been open to the public since the Saints had departed for the mountains. Some vandals tried to break in and actually wrote graffiti on the temple's outside walls. Within a few days of the incident a group of men had cleaned off the graffiti and then quietly and efficiently assembled a 12-foot-high metal fence on the sidewalk all the way around Temple Square, similar to the fences that had been constructed around many of the mountain camps. They also fenced off the blocks that held the Conference Center, the Joseph Smith Building and the Church Office Building.

The next group of thugs who tried to vandalize the temple discovered the hard way that the fence had been electrified. This put a quick stop to the vandalism.

A few weeks later arsonists burned the Jordan River Temple, and soon all of the temples received the same fencing. Tad wasn't sure who was putting them up, since all of the Saints were supposedly in the mountains, but Tad wasn't aware that before the migration to the mountains the Church had specifically called 300 men as "maintenance missionaries" who were living unnoticed in the Salt Lake Valley, blending in with the remaining citizens. These men served as the Church's "eyes on the streets" by keeping the Church leaders notified of any troublesome situations.

These missionaries were unknown to the world, but they were organized into districts and zones, and they even had a mission president who coordinated their actions. For example, he had directed them to buy the fencing for the temples at various stores along the Wasatch Front to avoid attracting attention, and then they met at a designated temple and assembled the fences at night without hardly being noticed. They were also watching over the ward meetinghouses and other Church properties.

As fall approached, the nation prepared to commemorate Patriot Day on September 11th in memory of the victims of the World Trade Center attack more than a decade earlier. There had been major national tragedies in the following years, but that day still marked a turning point in the history of the world. Many of the older people could still remember the seemingly carefree era "before 9/11" and it created a longing for "the good old days."

The citizens didn't realize they were on the verge of a series of events that would put 9/11 in the distant past forever.

CHAPTER 14

The year's weather had been really strange and unpredictable, particularly in regard to tropical storms and hurricanes. If the year's current pace continued, it would be the most active storm season since 2005 when 28 named storms had developed, including the devastating hurricanes Katrina, Rita, and Wilma.

However, the great storm that would change the world wasn't ever given an official name. When it was over, the simple words "The Storm" were all that needed to be said.

The storm first appeared in early September in the north Pacific Ocean near Russia's eastern coast. It was massive and seemed to just pop up out of nowhere. It acted a bit like a tropical storm, but it also demonstrated the characteristics of a winter storm. The world's weather experts were baffled by it.

The storm's outer edges battered Alaska before it barreled southward, swirling just off the West Coast. It quickly doubled in size and stretched from Oregon all the way down to southern California.

As the storm reached land, a monstrous tidal surge flooded hundreds of miles of shoreline. Damage from the flooding alone totaled in the billions of dollars, but the worst was yet to come. Reports began to come in from San Francisco and Los Angeles of the storm's deadly ferocity.

The key element of the storm was hurricane-force winds accompanied by large hailstones. The hail was being reported as big as baseballs in some areas, smashing through roofs, knocking down power lines, shredding limbs from trees, and destroying every type of crop just a month before harvest season. California's economy was devastated in less than a day, and most of the state was without electricity.

Tad had stayed tuned to the Weather Channel all evening, and the images that were shown were hard for him to comprehend. Several airplane crashes were reported because of the storm, and hundreds of people were killed. All flights to or from California were suspended indefinitely until the storm moved on.

Another report showed dozens of terrified children leaving Disneyland, where hailstones were piled a foot high in the pathways. However, Tad had to admit he enjoyed the report about the crazy surfers who rode the storm's incoming waves. One wide-eyed surfer said, "Dude, I got to ride the biggest wave of my life today. It had to be at least eighty feet tall. It took me past the beach and all the way to my apartment. My apartment's flooded now, but that ride was totally awesome!"

The forecasters expected the storm to weaken, but as it crossed the Sierra Nevada mountains, it seemed to strengthen even more. The following morning it had reached the Utah-Nevada border and the hailstones turned the bright neon signs of Wendover's casinos into thousands of glass shards, killing several people.

At around 11 a.m., Ken stuck his head into Tad's office. "Come on, you've got to see what's coming," he said.

Ken led Tad to the office buildings's top floor, where several other employees had gathered. They had a clear view to the west, where a pitch black cloud filled the horizon. They all watched in fascination as the cloud moved rapidly forward across the Great Salt Lake, which was churning wildly.

"I've never seen anything like it," Tad said.

Within five minutes the storm reached the city, and the seriousness of the situation became apparent. They watched in horror as large hailstones crashed through the windshields of cars on the roads below. One driver tried to run to safety but was pelted several times. He collapsed to the ground, and his motionless body was pulverized by the hail.

Within seconds the first hail pounded their building, and almost instantly a couple of hailstones shattered the plate-glass window. Everyone panicked and rushed for the doors. Since Tad was one of the last people to enter the room, he was able to dash down a stairway and get back to his office quickly, where he instinctively hid under his desk.

Hailstones battered his office window, and then one crashed through, bouncing against his leg. Tad grabbed it. The stone was solid ice and was the size of a grapefruit. It weighed at least five pounds.

"This is insane," he shouted, just as another one landed within five feet of him, bounced, and then shattered a photo he had kept on his desk of Emma and the kids. "I hope my family is surviving the storm better than I am," he said to himself.

It was a long, dark afternoon. The storm finally passed, and that evening he was able to return to his apartment, which had been badly damaged. The windows were smashed, and everything he owned was soaked.

The Church had used its satellite network to alert the leaders of the mountain camps of the approaching storm, and when it arrived they had buckled down and were well-prepared for it.

Thankfully, the mountains along the Wasatch Front acted as a good buffer against the storm, and the camps only received a two-hour dose of pea-sized hail. The storm definitely did some damage, but it was nothing like the hail that had ravaged the valleys.

Once the storm crossed over the Rocky Mountains, it regained strength over the open plains of eastern Colorado. The wheat and corn fields of Kansas and Nebraska were absolutely demolished, and the storm's rampage never let up again on its march across the United States. Two days later the storm walloped everywhere from Massachusetts to Florida, leaving the nation's upcoming fall harvest in ruins. The storm even moved on to batter Europe before fizzling out over Asia.

The storm's impact was completely devastating to the nation's crops. The storm couldn't have come at a worse time, since most of the crops had been fully ripe, such as the fruit, corn and wheat, and they would have been harvested within the next month. Now everything was ruined, and there wasn't enough time left in the growing season to replant anything before winter arrived.

One newspaper editorial had the headline, "Will we go hungry on Turkey Day?" The writer predicted that by Thanksgiving the United States would see the highest level of hunger among its citizens since the Great Depression in the 1930s.

As word reached the Jolley's Ranch camp of how destructive the hailstorm had been, Doug gathered the family together and told them about it.

"It is terrible that people are suffering today across the nation, but I am grateful for how the Lord is looking out for us," he said. "We have only been in the camp for about a month, and yet we have already been blessed. We were spared the worst of the hail, and while the rest of the nation scrambles to find anything to eat, we have plenty of food stored here."

Doug then invited the family members to open their scriptures to D&C 29:16.

"David, could you read that verse for us?" he asked.

David nodded. "It says, '*And there shall be a great hailstorm sent forth to destroy the crops of the earth.*'"

The group seemed surprised to find such a direct reference to the storm in the scriptures. Doug motioned toward the children in the group and said, "Someday you can tell your kids that you were alive when this verse was fulfilled."

CHAPTER 15

When Josh heard about the great hailstorm through the Church's network, he knew it would likely start the economic tailspin in the United States he had been told to watch for by Elder Smith. It could still be several months before the Quetzaltenango group would begin its journey, but Josh felt the time had finally come to tell the Saints what lay in store for them.

However, Josh realized the Saints under his direction needed to be reorganized. They were still living in makeshift groups that were somewhat aligned with their previous wards and stakes, but families were now moving around and getting lost in the shuffle. Some were even living outside the temple grounds in the buildings that had been repaired, and there had been a few reports of theft and heated arguments.

To begin the reorganization, Josh announced that every Saint should meet on the hill behind the temple the following Sunday morning, with no exceptions. It was time to put the group onto the pathway to Zion—both literally and figuratively.

As the Saints gathered that morning, Josh and Kim sat alone on a small stand positioned against the back wall of the temple. The temple workers had arranged a powerful speaker system that would reach everyone, and instrumental hymns played softly over the system as the Saints began to fill the hillside. They first came in small groups, but then it was like a flood of humanity as thousands gathered behind the temple.

As the final families arrived, Kim went to the podium and began singing "The Spirit of God." The group joined with her in unison, and the Spirit did indeed descend on the people.

When the song finished, one of the Guatemalan stake presidents gave a powerful opening prayer. Then Josh went to the podium. His Spanish was almost fluent, but he had prayed that on this special day, his language skills would rise to the occasion.

Josh welcomed them all and thanked them for the Christlike attitude they had shown during the hard times after the hurricane. He then said, "I have learned through the Church website that the United States has been struck with a great storm even larger than the one we experienced. Their economy is suffering, and there are reports of violence and other troubles. This is a great sign that the Second Coming of the Lord is soon approaching."

Josh stretched his arms wide and continued, "The time has come to share with you what lies ahead for this group. Maybe you have wondered why we have had you stay together at the temple rather than return to your homes. It is because you are a chosen people. You are going to fulfill the great promises found in the Book of Mormon that were given to your ancestors. If you prove to be faithful, this very group will help build New Jerusalem!"

The group was silent for a moment, but then light applause rippled through the crowd.

Josh smiled and said, "I know it is Sunday, but feel free to celebrate such wonderful news. It is a great opportunity, and I am thrilled to be here with you. Together we will soon journey to the place called Missouri in the United States and build a holy city to the Lord!"

Josh's enthusiasm transferred to the group, and this time they shouted and cheered.

"That's more like it," Josh said. "But we have much to do to prepare ourselves. It is a long journey, and so the time has come for us to organize ourselves more efficiently. In the past, we have been organized into wards based on where our homes were, but now we will organize you by family groups."

Josh had pondered and prayed how to best organize them, and the answer had come to follow the pattern of the Children of

Israel. In the Quetzaltenango group there were about 20 former or current stake presidents. He had prayed about each one of them, and had come up with the names of twelve men who would lead the new groups.

Josh continued, "We will organize ourselves like Moses did when he led the Twelve Tribes out of the land of Egypt. We have many powerful leaders in our group, but the Lord has selected twelve men to serve as the leaders of our own twelve tribes. I would like the following men to join me on the stand."

Josh then read the names, and when they had all joined him, he told the group, "These twelve men are true servants of the Lord. Through their years of service, they have shown their faithfulness, and I promise you that if you follow their example and guidance, you will be blessed."

Josh then assigned each of the men a number and told the crowd, "This number is how your family group will be identified as we prepare to travel to Missouri. Individual groups will be known as the First Stake, the Second Stake, and so on down to the Twelfth Stake. It doesn't matter whether you are first or twelfth, because we are all equal in the eyes of the Lord. This will just help us to stay organized."

Josh then asked the men to spread out about 100 feet apart in front of the group. "I would like the wives and children of these men to come join their fathers," Josh instructed.

A large number of people stood and moved down the hill, surrounding the men they were related to.

Josh then said, "Now it might get a little complicated, because I know some of you remaining on the hill are possibly the grandchildren to more than one of these men. But I would like all married sons to take their wives and children to the group where their parents are."

This took a few minutes to sort out, and there was a little confusion and raised voices when some of the wives wanted to join with their parents.

Josh took the microphone again. "I promise you won't be

separated from your families. We will still be living all together here on the temple grounds. This is simply so we can be better organized."

Josh's comments helped ease their fears, and soon the only people left on the hill were a few people who had been the only members of their families to join the Church. These remaining people were then assigned to certain groups to make the numbers as balanced as possible. There were about 15,000 people total, so each stake had around 1,200 members.

Josh took the microphone again and assigned each of the twelve new stakes a portion of the temple grounds. "We are all brothers and sisters in Christ, and great spiritual blessings await us if we are faithful. I know it would be a major challenge to move all of our belongings to new locations, so I ask that you use the shelters, food, and whatever else is on the land where you are now assigned. If you see someone's special keepsake, please put it aside and we will get everything sorted out. Please show kindness in all you do."

Josh then said, "A key reason we are reorganizing in this way is because we must be both physically and spiritually prepared for our journey. I know that many of you have never been inside the temple. The time has come for us to make sure that all worthy men are ordained to the Melchizedek Priesthood, and that all adults receive their temple ordinances. Then most importantly, we need to make sure every family is sealed together for eternity. That is the great work we will be doing for the next few weeks."

The crowd buzzed with excitement. The majority of them had lived in outlying areas where priesthood advancement and temple recommends had not been emphasized, especially since the temple was only recently completed. But Josh knew the people needed the blessings of the temple to achieve what awaited them.

Josh then dismissed them to their assigned areas of the temple grounds, and he was pleased to see them move happily to their new locations.

Josh turned to Kim and gave a sigh. "It just dawned on me what a huge task we have ahead of us," he said.

Kim smiled up at him. "Everything will work out. They are all very excited. When you said their families could be sealed for eternity, I felt a powerful surge of energy pass through them. They now have a goal, and I think we'll soon have our own little city of Zion right here."

That night Josh sent a lengthy report over the satellite network directly to Elder Smith explaining the stake reorganizations that had taken place and the goal they had set to have all the adults receive their temple ordinances before departing for Missouri.

Elder Smith soon responded, "Elder Brown, I can tell the Lord is working miracles through you. I reported your activities to the Quorum of the Twelve this morning, and we are all pleased with what you have accomplished. We will keep you posted on the situation here in the United States, which is quickly disintegrating. But the time has not yet arrived for you to begin your journey. There are several vital events that must still happen, so continue to focus on the members' spiritual preparation. We are praying for your success, and we know the Lord is with you."

❖ ❖ ❖

Once the newly organized stakes were settled into their areas, Josh met with each stake president to set him apart and help him choose his counselors. He also worked with each stake presidency to select four bishops and divide their stake into four wards.

Dozens of temple workers were called, set apart, and trained, and soon the temple was in full operation from 6 a.m. to 10 p.m. every day except Sunday. It turned out that only about 900 of the Saints had ever been to the temple before, leaving thousands of people who needed to receive their work.

Each stake was assigned one full day to be at the temple every two weeks, and the bishoprics and stake presidencies spent the other days busily interviewing people for recommends and organizing temple preparation classes.

Josh and Kim were constantly on the go every day, assisting the temple presidency in many ways. Kim spent a lot of time in the sealing rooms holding and comforting young children as they waited to be sealed to their parents. It was a glorious but exhausting assignment. One night as she and Josh collapsed into bed, she told him, "If we could somehow collect the energy of every wiggly child in the sealing rooms, we could probably fly to Missouri."

Josh smiled. "I'm sorry that your current assignment is more temporal than spiritual, but I know those mothers are very appreciative."

"Don't get me wrong," Kim said. "I love being in the temple every day, and it is wonderful to see these little families being sealed together. Some of the people have even seen angels in the room during the sealing, and I believe the angels are there—I just haven't had time to look around for them."

Josh nodded. "I know what you mean. It would be nice to be able to slow the pace, but it feels like we are racing against time. I have a new respect for what Brigham Young went through in early 1846 when he helped thousands of Saints receive their temple blessings in the final days before they left Nauvoo."

"That's true," Kim said, suddenly feeling a bit ashamed for complaining. "At least we don't have mobs trying to kill us like those early Saints did. I'd certainly rather be in my current situation, even if I have to change an occasional stinky diaper."

Josh laughed. "Yes, things could be worse."

⚜ ⚜ ⚜

The temple work was moving along extremely well. Each person who was attending the temple for the first time was given a card on which they wrote their personal information and the date each ordinance was completed. Once a person had received all of their ordinances, the card was given to a temple worker who entered the information and dates into the temple's computer data base.

Then each morning Josh would e-mail the previous day's batch of records to Church headquarters. It was an efficient system, and it assured that all this work wouldn't be lost once the group began the journey to New Jerusalem.

CHAPTER 16

The great hailstorm had taken an emotional toll on everyone in Salt Lake City, but Tad felt particularly depressed as he sat in his office. This was his first day back to work in more than a week.

The office building had suffered such severe damage that it had been off-limits until now, so he had spent a few days as a volunteer helping to clear tree limbs from the city streets. He hated to admit that he had enjoyed that job more than the one he actually got paid to do.

Besides, he didn't feel particularly safe being six stories in the air with only a sheet of plastic covering the hole where his window once was. The storm had shattered so many windows across the nation that the company told him to not expect a new one for several weeks. So he tolerated the slight breeze through his office and dug into the large pile of reports on his desk.

The damage reports from the storm were hard to comprehend. Ninety percent of the nation's wheat, corn and citrus crop was destroyed, and the government predicted major food shortages in the coming months. People had naturally rushed to the stores to stock up on whatever food was left, but there wasn't much to go around. Tad was glad he only had himself to feed, and he had enough food in his cupboards to last for a couple of weeks. He was also grateful that his apartment had sustained only minor damage, and so he was much better off than some of his co-workers.

What surprised Tad the most was the upbeat attitude that his boss Ken was showing. Just that morning Ken had told him, "Don't worry, Tad. The world will always need accountants, even if we are just counting up their losses." But Tad felt Ken was being too optimistic. Some of their key accounts were companies that might not ever recover from the storm.

That night as Tad lay in bed his mind was filled with worst-case scenarios. "If the economy fails, then I'm out of a job, and I'll have to use up my savings to stay afloat, and I'll never be able to buy Emma a house, so she'll never come back to me, and I'll never see my kids again, and I'll always be alone, and . . ."

He sat up in bed and screamed in agony. It felt like he was inside a whirlpool and was getting sucked into a dark abyss. The sense of panic literally paralyzed him for several minutes. When he had sufficiently recovered, he felt compelled to have his savings in his hands and then hidden in a safe place.

It was after midnight when he hurried out of his apartment building and went to an ATM machine outside a nearby bank, where he tried to withdraw all $10,000 in his savings account. The ATM would only allow him to withdraw a maximum of $500. He banged on the machine with his fist and shouted, "Come on! It's my money!"

Tad finally went ahead and withdrew the $500 from the ATM. He then tried again, but the machine wouldn't allow another transaction to go through. "That will have to do for now," he told himself, not wanting to draw any extra attention to his account.

He returned to his apartment, but the feeling kept eating at him that he needed to withdraw his savings. He needed to be at work before the bank opened, but during his lunch break he walked two blocks to the nearest branch of his bank.

He filled out the withdrawal slip and handed it to the teller, who looked at the slip and scrunched up her nose.

"How come you didn't just go online and transfer the money directly to your chip?" she asked.

Tad shook his head. "I want the money in cash. There should be $9,500 in my savings account."

The teller looked surprised. "Okay. But I will need to talk to my manager about any large cash transactions."

She went to her manager's office, and the man soon came to the counter. "Hello. I understand you want to make a cash withdrawal rather than just having the money available through your chip?"

"Yes, I would like my current savings balance in cash."

The manager frowned. "That's an unusual request. We hardly make any cash transactions now."

"I know everyone uses their chips now, but is it illegal to carry around cash?" Tad asked, getting impatient.

"No, but you're putting yourself at risk of robbery or simply losing the money—"

"I completely understand, but that is what I would like to do. Why is it so hard to let me withdraw my own money?"

"You are right. I apologize," the manager said. He turned to the cashier's computer and called up Tad's account. "It looks like you have $9,500 in savings. Would you like to withdraw it all?"

"Yes. I'll take it in $20 bills."

"Go ahead and do as Mr. North has requested," the manager told the cashier, who was looking at Tad like he was a circus freak.

The cashier soon counted out the money and put it into a small canvas bag for him.

Tad headed back to his office, where he had a briefcase that held the additional $500 he had withdrawn the night before. He closed the office door and put all of the money in the briefcase. As he locked the briefcase, the darkness that had filled him since the night before ebbed away. He wasn't sure why he had withdrawn the money, but he knew it was the right thing to do.

In some ways, the thought of having $10,000 sitting next to him was almost unbelievable. He and Emma had scraped and saved for so many years and had never been able to get ahead. Now within a few months he had more money than he knew what to do with.

The next four hours at work dragged on forever, but finally at 5 p.m. Tad grabbed the briefcase and went straight to his car. He knew he couldn't rest until the money was safely tucked away. Emma had once showed him a piece of loose concrete in the cellar floor in her parents' home in Springville where she had hidden her allowance money when she was a child. Now Tad would use that same hiding place to protect their savings.

He arrived at the Daltons' home that evening and first went inside to make sure no one else was there. Then he took the briefcase into the cellar and removed the piece of loose concrete. The briefcase fit perfectly into the gap behind it. He put the concrete back in place and then took some bottled cherries that Emma's parents had left behind and stacked them on top of the hiding place. He even gathered some dust from a shelf and sprinkled it over the bottles.

Finally he stepped back and admired his work. "Nice job," he said. "It looks like those bottles have been there for 20 years."

He returned to his apartment and slept better than he had in several months.

✦ ✦ ✦

The next morning Tad entered his office and logged on to his computer. A message popped up that read, "*Invalid Password.*"

"Come on, I've entered it a thousand times," Tad said to himself. He tried it twice more with the same response.

"Great," he muttered. "Just what I need."

He went to the front desk and told the secretary, "My computer won't let me log in. Has anyone else had problems?"

She shook her head. "Nope, just you. I think you need to talk to Ken."

"What is this about?"

The secretary just tilted her head toward Ken's office. "Just go see him."

Tad walked down to Ken's office and found his boss meeting with a man Tad had never seen before.

Ken nodded to him and looked a bit rattled. "Tad, I'd like you to meet Officer Jonas Fernelius from the CCA. He has a couple of questions for you."

Tad's stomach suddenly started to hurt. The CCA—The Chip Compliance Authority—was a new government agency that tracked any unusual behavior by people who had the chip. There had already been some reports of excessive force being used by CCA officers on people who violated the government's ever-growing list of chip-related policies. Tad had talked to several people who felt the CCA was pushing the country toward martial law, but they didn't dare speak too much about it and risk becoming targets themselves.

Tad swallowed hard as he shook hands with the officer, who was dressed casually in a button-down blue shirt and khaki pants. But the officer's shaved head and goatee added to the intimidation factor and indicated he was all business.

"It's nice to meet you," Tad said with a quiver in his voice. "How can I help you?"

Officer Fernelius patted him on the shoulder. "There's no reason to be nervous, Mr. North. I just wanted to talk to you about the large cash withdrawals you made that emptied your savings account."

Tad shrugged. "I'm thinking about making a down payment on a house and wanted to have it handy."

"Good for you," the officer said. "I like to see people making a step forward in life. But I'm wondering why you needed the money in cash. Wouldn't the title company prefer to use your chip and transfer the money electronically?"

"I suppose so, but I guess I'm a bit old-fashioned. I like to keep my money close at hand."

Officer Fernelius laughed. "You're funny, Mr. North. 'Close at hand.' All you had to do was use the chip in your hand."

Officer Fernelius stared at Tad for a few seconds before unexpectedly shoving him against the wall. Ken instinctively stepped forward to pull them apart, but the officer pointed at him and said, "Sit down in your chair and don't move. This is between me and Mr. North."

Ken did as he was told, and the officer got right in Tad's face. "It's time to quit messing around with me," he hissed. "I know everything about you. We've been monitoring your chip for weeks, waiting for you to slip up."

"What are you talking about?" Tad asked. "All I do is come to work and go to an occasional Gladiatorzz game."

Officer Fernelius looked furious. "Oh, is that all? I believe you are still legally married to a woman who fled into the mountains with a Mormon non-conformist group from Springville. I would hate to discover the $10,000 has somehow found its way to that group, because you would suddenly be in a lot of hot water."

"I promise it hasn't!" Tad cried. "I haven't seen my wife and kids in several weeks."

Officer Fernelius shoved Tad to the floor and shouted, "Liar! Your chip's GPS system shows you went to your in-laws' house in Springville yesterday. Who did you meet there?"

"Nobody!"

"Then where is the money? Two of our officers spent an hour searching that house early this morning and couldn't find it."

Tad was growing frustrated. "You had no right to do that. That's private property."

"I'm sorry, but that house belongs to someone who is associated with a renegade group," Officer Fernelius said. "It's fair game."

Tad was silent, and the officer continued to berate him. "I know you attended a meeting at an LDS church in West Jordan recently. Do you still consider yourself a member of that religion?"

"I do."

"Well, I always admire a man who stands up for his beliefs," Officer Fernelius said. "But let me be straight with you. Your actions look suspicious and I have the authority to lock you up until the money is accounted for. I need you to return the $10,000 to your savings account today, or you'll be spending time in the county jail. Have I made myself clear?"

"Don't worry, I'll get the money back into the account."

"Very good," the officer said. "Oh, and there is one other thing. As part of this agreement, I need you to make an oath that you no longer consider yourself a member of the LDS Church."

Tad turned to Ken in shock. "Have you made an oath?"

Ken looked at the floor. "I have."

"Why? I can't believe you would turn against the Church!"

Ken tried to justify his decision. "Tad, it's the only way to survive. The Church is disintegrating, but our company is thriving. Life is good. Trust me, we'll take good care of you. That $10,000 will soon feel like small change. Just make the oath and we'll forget this ever happened."

Tad felt completely betrayed, and he no longer had any desire to work for Ken. The money suddenly didn't matter at all. Tad could see what an idiot he had been, knowing he should be at the camp with his family. But he also knew he now had to keep his cool and act carefully if he was going to stay out of jail.

"Okay, you've got me figured out," he told the officer. "As you suspected, the money is in Springville. I'll drive down there and bring it back this afternoon."

Officer Fernelius smiled. "Do I look stupid? I'll drive you there myself. I'll even drive you to the bank afterward!"

Within a few minutes they were on I-15 in Officer Fernelius' black Ferrari. "Nice car," Tad said. "I have a 2009 Porsche, but it doesn't come close to this."

"Yeah, they treat us pretty good in this job," Officer Fernelius said. "Plus, I don't have to worry about speeding tickets."

He gunned the engine and soon hit 110 miles an hour, making Tad's heart leap. The officer spent the next few minutes talking about his driving exploits while Tad plotted his next move. He had figured out an escape plan, but the difficulty he faced was that the chip in his hand would pinpoint wherever he went. Even if he got away, Officer Fernelius would immediately be on his trail.

They took the north Springville freeway off-ramp and stopped at the red light, waiting to cross the overpass. They were in the middle of a long line of cars, and Tad knew the time had come.

As the Ferrari turned east and began to climb the overpass, Tad asked the officer another question about the Ferrari to distract him. Then Tad unbuckled his seatbelt, opened the door, leapt over a three-foot concrete barrier, and tumbled down the side of the overpass.

It happened so quickly that Officer Fernelius actually kept talking for a moment. Then he slammed on the brakes, but a big dumptruck right behind him crashed into the back of the Ferrari and then settled on top of it, temporarily trapping Officer Fernelius inside.

Tad rolled to a stop at the bottom of the overpass and looked up long enough to see the mayhem he had caused. Then he sprinted toward a grove of trees west of the freeway. As he entered the grove, he glanced back and saw Officer Fernelius standing on the overpass. The officer had been delayed long enough by the accident that he hadn't actually seen which direction Tad had gone, but he was now pointing a handheld device straight in his direction.

"Great, he's tracking me," Tad said. "I'm a dead man."

Tad's heart started pounding furiously. He spotted a broken beer bottle lying on the ground. He picked it up and plunged the bottle's jagged edge into the back of his right hand. As blood spurted out, Tad tried to locate the chip. It was embedded deeper than he thought, and horrible pain shot through his right arm as he pinched the chip between the thumb and forefinger of his left hand. It didn't want to come easily, because the flesh had grown around it, but in a frenzy he ripped it out.

He glanced at the bloody item to make sure it was indeed the chip, then he threw it about 20 yards back toward the freeway, hoping to buy some time before Officer Fernelius closed in. He wrapped his bleeding hand in his shirt and ran through waist-high brush toward Utah Lake. After about a mile, he reached the lake and crouched down in the water so only his head was showing.

Tad looked back in the direction he had come and didn't see anyone on his trail. He breathed a big sigh of relief, even though he knew the federal charges against him were piling up quickly. Just the unauthorized removal of his chip alone would land him a lengthy prison sentence and the confiscation of his belongings.

He checked his hand, and it was looking pretty gross. He tore off another part of his shirt and tightly wrapped his hand again. Finally the bleeding stopped.

"Heavenly Father, I thank thee for sparing my life," he prayed. Then he started to laugh. Here he was, neck-deep in a dirty lake with a gaping cut in his hand that would probably get infected. He had no food, no family, no job, and now he was a wanted fugitive.

He looked up at the sky and said, "Lord, I get the picture! I'm an idiot. So either let me die quickly like I deserve, or help me find a way back to my family."

He waited quietly for some sort of answer, but there was only silence.

Tad stayed hidden along the eastern shore of Utah Lake for two days as he worked his way south. He didn't dare go into Springville or Spanish Fork, sensing that his face was being shown on the local news broadcasts and in the newspapers. He had been drinking the lake water out of desperation, but he needed some food soon.

As the sun began to set during his second night of hiding, the lights of Lincoln Point, a new housing development across the lake on West Mountain, beckoned to him. Tad knew the lake really wasn't too deep, and he decided to cross the lake to Lincoln Point. Surely there would be a city park where he could find some leftovers in a garbage can.

His journey across the lake was uneventful. It took a couple of hours, but he only had to swim for a little while and was able to wade most of the way. He came ashore in Lincoln Point around midnight and made his way to the center of the little community. He located the city park and dug through the garbage cans, where he found a half-eaten box of Chicken McNuggets and four stale donuts. They tasted great.

The city park's bathrooms were locked, but Tad managed to scale the fence of the community swimming pool and get into the shower room. He showered off and scrubbed his clothes the best he could, but he still smelled faintly like a mix of lake sludge and rotting fish.

Plus, his shirt was so blood-stained that he shredded it and flushed it down a toilet. He knew Officer Fernelius wasn't going to let him get away easily, and there were probably news bulletins about him, so he had to stay out of sight. He was certain they would have easily located his discarded chip, so a bloody shirt would have been a good hint of his whereabouts.

Tad rummaged though the locker room and found a blue sweatsuit, some socks, and some nice tennis shoes. They were a couple of sizes too big for him, but at least they were dry. A tinge of guilt filled him as he changed into the clothes, but he felt he had no choice. "Heavenly Father, go ahead and add 'thievery' to my list of sins," he said. "Don't worry, I'm going to get back on track soon."

Now that he had some decent clothes, he went to a sink and unwrapped his injured hand. It still looked ghastly and wasn't healing very well. There was some infection that he cleaned out, but he really needed about six stitches. He grimaced as he wrapped it tightly again with a sock and tried to block out the pain.

Just then a car door slammed outside the building. Tad unbolted a side door and ran into the darkness of the park. He saw a young couple get out of the car and sit at a picnic table near the building. It looked like they planned to stay awhile, so he needed to go somewhere else to avoid being seen.

He thought about going back to the lake, but he was tired of being wet. He decided his best option would be to climb West Mountain and find a hiding place. It would give him a good vantage point to watch for Officer Fernelius and allow him to sneak back down into the city at night to search for food.

By sunrise Tad was halfway up the north side of the mountain. He found a small cavern and decided to make it his home. He sat at the cavern's entrance and watched as the morning sunlight backlit Mount Timpanogos on the other side of the valley. It was a beautiful scene. He really wished Emma had been there to share it with him.

CHAPTER 17

Five days after escaping from Officer Fernelius, Tad was still hiding in his cavern on West Mountain. He had seen a lot of police activity around the community pool the day after his shower. He figured he must have left some evidence of his visit. He remembered flushing his shirt down the toilet, but he had no recollection of what he had done with his shoes and pants when he changed into the sweatsuit.

His suspicions were confirmed when a dark suburban with a CCA logo on the side had spent an hour there. He was pretty sure Officer Fernelius was the one who climbed out of the driver's seat. "He's probably just as mad about getting his Ferrari smashed and having to drive that thing as he is about my escape," Tad told himself.

Knowing that the authorities were searching for him made it almost impossible to sleep. He felt sure if he closed his eyes, he would wake up with Officer Fernelius staring down at him. He mainly sat quietly all day at the cavern opening, talking to himself about his actions the past few weeks. Humiliation washed over him as he thought of everything he had thrown away. He had lost the trust of his beautiful wife and loving children, and for what?

"Dear Heavenly Father, I've been such a fool," he prayed. "I can't believe what I've done. I thought I was so smart, but look what I've become—a hermit living in a cave who is hiding from the law. Please give me another chance. I was swayed and tempted by the ways of the world at the worst possible time. Please open the way for me to rejoin my family."

His heart literally hurt, and his whole body seemed engulfed in pain for the choices he had made. He curled up in a ball on the cavern's hard, uneven floor and sobbed himself to sleep.

When the walls of the cavern began shaking later that day, Tad first attributed it to his mental state. He hadn't eaten in nearly a week, and he could hardly see straight. But when a large rock cracked away from the cavern wall and bounced off his foot, he knew this wasn't a hallucination.

He scrambled outside and clung to the side of the ridge as the cavern collapsed on itself. The shaking continued for another thirty seconds and dislodged a couple of large boulders that cascaded down the mountainside directly at Tad. He crouched behind an outcropping as they hurtled over his head.

Finally the shaking stopped. Tad knew it was the strongest earthquake he had ever felt, and could even have been "The Big One." He noticed plumes of smoke beginning to rise across the lake in Provo, while down below, he could see the people of Lincoln Point emerging like ants from their homes.

A few minutes later there was an aftershock that sent everyone scurrying, but then Tad saw an amazing sight across the valley. A wall of water was pouring out of Provo Canyon. From his vantage point on West Mountain, it looked like someone had turned on a gigantic garden hose at the mouth of the canyon.

The water funneled its way through Provo, quickly reaching the NuSkin Building and spreading into southern Provo's East Bay shopping district.

Tad could tell this wasn't a minor flood. The water soon reached Utah Lake and created a large wave that rushed directly toward Lincoln Point. He watched as homes below him were pounded and then covered by water as if they were toys in a sloshing bathtub. After the initial surge, the water receded and began to fan out throughout the valley.

Tad tried to figure out where so much water could have come

from, finally saying to himself, "The dam at Deer Creek Reservoir must have burst."

The flood was actually the water from two reservoirs. The earthquake had first affected Jordanelle Reservoir, located a few miles east of Park City. The quake had split the dam and sent millions of gallons of water roaring through Heber City and into Deer Creek Reservoir.

The tidal wave of water had engulfed and overflowed Deer Creek Dam, causing it to swiftly erode. Five minutes after the initial wave of water, a deep gash had emerged down the center of the dam. Before anyone could even send a warning, the water of two full reservoirs was channeled into Provo Canyon, creating a towering wall of water that obliterated everything in the canyon.

As the initial flood surge settled, Tad looked all around him. Some of the water had nearly reached Payson, and the BYU campus looked like a distant shoreline, with the Kimball Tower appearing to be a lighthouse overlooking the flooded valley.

Within an hour, Utah Lake was six feet deeper and had temporarily doubled in size. The added water turned the Jordan River near Lehi into a massive torrent that tore through the narrow gap at the Point of the Mountain, flooding low-lying areas in the Salt Lake Valley as the water journeyed to the Great Salt Lake.

Tad's immediate concern was his right foot, which had been injured by the falling rock. He carefully took his shoe off and checked to see what was wrong. It didn't feel like he had broken any bones, but the foot throbbed from his big toe to above his ankle. As the shock of the earthquake and the flood wore off, the pain seemed to intensify and there was also some swelling. As he put the shoe back on, he was thankful the shoes he had found had been two sizes too big, because now that shoe fit very well.

Tad watched as the residents of Lincoln Point began sorting through their shattered homes. He felt terrible for the people who had been affected by the disaster, but he realized he had been given a second chance. He hoped Officer Fernelius would now have more urgent tasks to worry about than tracking him down, but he still felt he should stay clear of interacting with anyone or asking for a ride, knowing it could backfire and land him in jail.

He looked eastward toward Hobble Creek Canyon. If he was going to ever be with his family again, he needed to somehow get there. The flood would force him to first go south for several miles almost to Payson, but nothing was going to stop him now. He could only laugh at his situation, though. With a sliced-up right hand and a smashed right foot, it was going to be a slow journey.

Despite his physical problems, he truly felt grateful. If he hadn't withdrawn his savings, he would have still been in Salt Lake with a chip in his hand. "Thank you, Heavenly Father," he prayed. "I am grateful for the protection I have received this day. I know I didn't deserve a second chance, but I'm going to make the most of it."

He started limping down the mountain, but he stopped in his tracks as he felt a response from heaven. "*You have been granted this chance because of the faith and prayers of your wife and children. You must now change your life and honor your priesthood once again.*"

Tad nodded grimly. "I will, Lord. I will."

CHAPTER 18

The camp at Jolley's Ranch suffered some damage from the earthquake, such as a broken water line and a few walls falling off the pavilion. But the tents had just swayed back and forth, and overall there wasn't much to clean up. The camp members figured it had been just a medium-sized tremor, but as they began to receive reports though the stake president's laptop, the earthquake's true magnitude sunk in.

The earthquake had been centered near Park City and was being categorized as a 7.2 on the Richter scale. That jolt is what had split the Jordanelle Dam and started the terrible chain of events throughout central Utah.

The Church network had links to several news clips about the earthquake. One clip showed a reporter at a TV news bureau located at University Avenue and 500 North in Provo soon after the flood hit. He was standing on the building's two-story roof, and the swirling brown water was only a few feet below him.

"This is easily the worst disaster Provo has ever experienced," the reporter said in the clip. "Nearly every building within my sight is devastated."

The camera panned around him, showing large trees floating by and people huddled on housetops. Across the street from him was the Provo City Library, which despite being surrounded by water seemed to be holding up pretty well. As the camera showed the library, dozens of people could be seen peering out the windows from the upper rooms.

Doug shook his head in awe. "I doubt the water got that deep in Springville, but if that is what downtown Provo looked like, our houses definitely got soaked."

As the days rolled on, the camp continued to receive terrible news, not just from Utah, but from across the United States. It seemed like a decade's worth of natural disasters had been unleashed in just a few weeks. It was being called "The Autumn of Destruction." There were unexpected earthquakes in New England, volcanoes in the Northwest, tornadoes throughout the Plains states, major wildfires throughout the Southwest, and strong hurricanes coming ashore along the Atlantic coast and in the Gulf of Mexico.

The biggest story by far, though, was the earthquake that struck near Las Vegas. It made the Utah quake look small. Many of the huge hotels along the Las Vegas Strip buckled and crumbled. The news reports showed over and over a video of the miniature version of the Statue of Liberty that had stood along the Strip toppling into the street and crushing two cars.

But like the Utah quake, the biggest loss came through a dam failure, this time at Lake Mead. The massive Hoover Dam survived the quake, but a hill along the lake's shore didn't. The hill had split open and formed a large sinkhole. It was a spectacular sight to see billions of gallons of water rushing down the opening. There was no way anyone could stop it, and within days nearly all of the lake had drained into this newly formed cavern. Scientists kept watching for the water to emerge elsewhere, but it simply disappeared into the earth.

There were a few other water sources in the area such as wells, but they were quickly claimed and controlled by armed groups, leaving the general public without any drinking water.

The impact of this catastrophe was felt throughout the West. In the midst of an unseasonably warm fall, California was now without one of its most important water sources. Restrictions were made throughout California on water usage, and tensions among citizens were running high.

Las Vegas itself became parched almost overnight. The daytime temperatures were more than 100 degrees, and the water supplies in the casinos and hotels were quickly gone. Hysteria filled the streets, and there were many murders committed as people carjacked vehicles in hopes of getting out of the city.

Many people tried driving south to California but ran out of gas in the desert. Others headed north toward Utah, but the earthquake had destroyed I-15 through the Virgin River Gorge. The old highway through Santa Clara was also damaged beyond repair, and the gruesome suffering from the heat and the violence among those who were stranded along the roadways was worse than any movie could have portrayed.

Very few people survived the exodus from Las Vegas, and those who did were emotionally scarred for life. Nearly all of the faithful members of the Church in the Las Vegas area had gone to gathering places far from the city and were spared the destruction.

Becky was particularly devastated by the news coming out of Nevada and California. Her parents had contacted her via e-mail through the Church network just two days before the Las Vegas earthquake. They had decided to leave their gathering place at the San Diego Temple and travel to the Jolley's Ranch Camp. Becky and Josh were their only children, and since Josh was in Guatemala, they had wanted to join Becky's family.

As the days passed without hearing from them, Becky figured they had been on I-15 somewhere near Las Vegas at the time of the earthquake. She feared the worst, and she was almost unable to function. Doug arranged for President Johnson to meet with her, and the president did his best to comfort her, but it was one of those situations that simply didn't make sense.

"If they had just stayed in San Diego, they would have been fine," Becky cried. "They said they felt inspired that they should come here, and now they are probably dead. Is that really what the Lord wanted?"

President Johnson could only say, "I honestly don't know. All I can say is if they were righteous people, they will have earned a place in the Celestial Kingdom, no matter what might have happened here on earth."

Becky still felt confused, but she knew all she could do is turn it over to the Lord and try to move on. The president let her send an e-mail each day to her parents, but there never was a response.

The disasters continued to pile up in the United States, but Mexico was even harder hit by volcanoes and hurricanes. Thousands of people had poured across the southern U.S. border and were causing all kinds of havoc.

With such disruptions, the government began using the chip as a way to keep control, and a form of martial law had been implemented. Chip-scanning checkpoints were set up throughout every major U.S. city, and anyone without a chip was considered an illegal alien and also as a potential terrorist threat.

These people were immediately detained by CCA officers and taken to "reconditioning centers" where they would be brutally interrogated as to why they didn't have a chip. If the answer was unsatisfactory—such as a religious belief—the person would be sent to the equivalent of a concentration camp.

This new pronouncement obviously had repercussions for all Church members in the United States. The Church leaders asked all of the undercover "maintenance missionaries" to retreat to the closest mountain camp as soon as possible, since the CCA checkpoints were usually random and the chance of getting caught was high.

There were reports that one of the concentration camps had been established at the Kennecott Copper Mine to the west of Salt Lake City. The mine was a massive pit hundreds of feet deep that served as a natural prison. The pit could hold thousands of prisoners without any real effort. The prisoners were just transported to the bottom of the pit with no shelter and basically left to fend for themselves. Twice a day the guards would use a catapult to launch a few boxes of water and food supplies into the pit. They really didn't care whether the prisoners starved to death or not, but it was really entertaining to watch them fight like dogs over the food and water. The guards would pull out their binoculars and have a grand time watching the battles. A few of the prisoners were clearly stronger and more malicious than the others, and they typically collected the most food each day.

In contrast, many prisoners feared for their lives and didn't want to take part in the violence. They would usually go find a spot away from everyone else and slowly waste away.

Enough captives were dying that every couple of days the guards would drive a dumptruck into the pit and force a few unlucky prisoners to gather up the bodies. Then the dumptruck would empty its load in a certain spot that was nicknamed "Mormon Hill." The guards would force the prisoners at gunpoint to cover the bodies with dirt by hand. It was a horrible task, and many prisoners secretly wished they could trade places with the deceased.

As word spread of this brutal inhumanity, the First Presidency asked each camp to send out two priesthood holders into their former communities to check for any possible members who had experienced a change of heart and who could be spared from such a fate.

The letter from the First Presidency stated, *"We issue this pronouncement with the realization that it might be greeted with mixed feelings. We realize that the time of preparation is long past, but we also believe in the Savior's admonition to seek after the lost sheep. If you feel your area's situation is too dangerous to attempt such a mission, then do not do so.*

"However, if there is a chance that you could go into your city and return safely, then follow the promptings of the Spirit in finding these precious souls. We feel there are possibly hundreds of our brothers and sisters who have been sufficiently humbled and will return to Christ if

we extend a loving hand at this time before it is everlastingly too late for them."

The First Presidency's pronouncement was indeed met with mixed emotions. One man said, "Anyone who is still down there had a chance to be here. All we need is to have those ungrateful 'cell phone girls' back in camp."

There were several other opinions given, but finally the stake president said, "If anyone is still left down there who wants to join us, their lives have been a lot worse than ours have been for the past few months. The only real question is whether we feel it is safe to send anyone down there."

Doug raised his hand. "I think if we had someone ride an ATV down there, it would be worth the effort. That way we will have followed the First Presidency's counsel, and we wouldn't have to worry about whether we neglected someone who needed our help."

President Johnson nodded. "I agree with you. I also feel you are the person who should go."

Doug was shocked. "Me? I'm not sure about that."

But then his father Mark came forward. "I don't want you going alone. We can go together on the ATV. We have plenty of gasoline stored here. We might as well use some of it."

President Johnson was pleased. "Thank you, Brother Dalton. That is courageous of you."

Within a few minutes Doug and Mark were on the ATV waving good-bye to the other camp members. Emma, Becky and Michelle had tried to talk them out of it, arguing that they had families to look after, but Mark pointed out that so did all of the other men. "Don't worry," Mark said. "We'll be back before sundown."

They rode the ATV down the canyon trail and followed Canyon Road to 400 South. They decided to head west, and as they reached the bottom of the hill near Ream's Supermarket, they received a shock. Taped to a light pole was a "wanted" poster that showed the names and photos of several men, including themselves!

The other names on the list included most of the men in their camp. Doug pulled the sign off the pole and folded it up. "This will give everyone at the camp a good laugh," he said.

The floodwaters had reached this part of town, but it didn't look like there was any attempt to clean things up.

Doug and Mark drove west to Main Street and traveled past Springville's city office complex, but it looked abandoned. As far as they could tell, the city was no longer functioning. The mayor and most of the city council had resigned their positions and gone with their stakes to the mountains, and it looked like they hadn't been replaced. They drove past the stake's meetinghouses and even looked inside, but they were also empty.

They even checked the homes of the families that had left the camp. Doug was admittedly curious to see how the "cell phone girls" were holding up in the muddy conditions, but it looked like they had hastily packed up and left when the flood came.

Doug wasn't surprised. The reports coming through the Church network indicated that several Utah County cities that had once been strong LDS communities were now ghost towns. Most citizens had either joined the mountain camps or had moved south to cities such as Nephi and Fillmore that hadn't been affected by the flood. Since Springville was without electricity, there hadn't been much of a reason for the people to stay, especially when they could get really good foreclosure deals in those other cities on homes that had been abandoned by faithful LDS families.

Before returning to the camp, Doug and Mark decided to travel past their own homes on the slim chance that Tad had shown up there. On Doug's door was an eviction notice from the bank, which made him laugh. "Judging by the layer of mud on the yard and the cobwebs in the windows, I think it should be pretty obvious I'm not spending much time here," he said.

But they were a bit alarmed when they arrived at Mark's house and saw the mess in the driveway. Somebody had dismantled Emma's minivan and taken the engine and frame, leaving a pile of parts. They had also put the old family Volkswagen up on blocks and taken the tires.

"Wow, people must be getting desperate if they wanted those car parts so badly," Doug said.

They suddenly missed the safety of the campground, and they started up the road feeling unsafe for the first time. Thankfully they were on their guard, because on the next block someone emerged from a house and ran toward them. It was Doug's old neighbor, Barry Newton, the man Doug had shared a laugh with in the church parking lot just a few months earlier when the buses departed. However, judging by the hatchet Barry was carrying in his hand, this wasn't going to be a friendly reunion.

"Doug Dalton, stop where you are," Barry roared. "There's a bounty on your head!"

Doug gunned the ATV just before Barry reached them. Barry threw the hatchet and it clanged off the back of the ATV, barely missing Mark's hand. Barry picked up the hatchet then stood in the road and cursed at them.

"I'm starting to think all of my home-teaching visits with Barry didn't really sink in," Doug told his dad.

"Wait," Mark responded. "We didn't invite him to the camp."

Doug gave his dad a strange look. "Are you serious?"

Mark laughed. "No. If we had extended to Barry a loving hand of fellowship, he would have chopped it off."

When they returned to camp, the members were impressed with the "wanted" poster. The members also were a little surprised at how abandoned the city was and that they hadn't brought anyone else with them.

Deep down, Emma was hoping they would be bringing back at least one person, but Doug took her aside and said, "Sorry, but we didn't see any sign of Tad."

There had been some private talk among the stake leaders that their group would soon be joining a larger group at the Manti Temple. Since they had traveled to the canyon by bus, they now had a real shortage of vehicles to transport their personal gear.

David had overheard some of these conversations, and an idea formed in his head. Now that the Hobble Creek Golf Course was abandoned, he figured there were a lot of now-useless golf carts just sitting at the abandoned golf clubhouse. He asked President Johnson if he could turn the golf carts into handcarts, similar to what the Mormon Pioneers had used to cross the Plains on their way to Utah in the 1800s.

The stake president didn't think it would hurt, so he gave David permission to give it a try. Doug, David, and a few other men went to the clubhouse and found the golf carts. Their batteries were dead, but the men pushed two of the carts back to the campground so David could experiment with them.

David quickly learned how to disassemble the carts and then reconfigure them so that they had more ground clearance and could easily be pushed or pulled. He came up with two different cart designs, and then he asked President Johnson to evaluate them.

President Johnson arrived that afternoon expecting to see a fairly amateur handcart. But when he saw David's two versions, he was very impressed. He grabbed one of the carts by the handle and moved it up and down a nearby hill.

"Wow, David, this cart works great," President Johnson said. He tried the other design but liked the first version the best.

"How many golf carts are still down at the clubhouse?" the president asked.

"Around 40," David said.

"Then I want to order 39 more handcarts just like that first one," President Johnson said with a smile. "And I also have a request."

"Certainly," David responded.

"I want you to write up how you modified these carts. I'm sure there are other LDS camps located near golf courses, and your design needs to be shared with them. Take a digital photo of the cart, and when you get me the written plans, I'll e-mail them to Church headquarters. I'll make sure they know it was David North of the Jolley's Ranch camp that came up with the idea."

David was very excited about the project, and they brought the rest of the carts to the camp. Also, the design plans were sent to the Church. Within a week President Johnson received a message back from one of the General Authorities, and he read it to the entire stake on Sunday.

The e-mail read, "President Johnson, thank you for sending the cart design. It looks very functional, and we are going to pass it along to all other Church units to use as they see fit. Please let David North know we are proud of what he has created."

David couldn't stop smiling for a solid week.

CHAPTER 19

Tad's journey from West Mountain to Springville took much longer than he had expected. Before the flood and without his injuries, Tad could have made the journey in less than a day. But the flood had traveled all the way to Payson, and even the roads were covered with mud. So he kept limping along West Mountain's foothills until he could finally find dry ground.

Three days into his journey he had finally circled around through Payson and Salem, and had reached Spanish Fork. His mind had become numb to the cries of frustrated families whose homes had been flooded and the general turmoil in the cities. He heard snatches of conversations, and many people seemed eager to just pack up and head south rather than deal with the damage caused by the flood.

Meanwhile, he just kept plodding along the sidewalk, and no one even acknowledged him. He could tell he was growing weaker by the hour, though. As the sun began to set, he collapsed under a tree in Spanish Fork's city park and slept like a rock the entire night.

When he awoke the next morning, he knew something wasn't right. His right arm had shooting pains, and his right foot was so swollen that he couldn't bend his ankle. At this rate, he would be lucky to make it to Springville, much less all the way up the canyon to where his family was camped.

"This is ridiculous," he said. As he pondered his situation, he knew he needed medical attention, but he also knew that as soon as he stepped inside a doctor's office, they would want identification.

If he provided it, Officer Fernelius would likely be there within a few minutes.

The thought formed in his mind that maybe if he could retrieve the $10,000 he had hidden in the Daltons' cellar, a doctor might treat him without asking any questions. There was a medical clinic just a few blocks from the Daltons' home where he could get help. He figured even if the building was abandoned, he might be able to find some painkillers there.

Tad's biggest concern now, however, was getting to Springville. No one was driving their cars because of the debris in the roads, so hitching a ride wasn't an option. Then he noticed a small bicycle on the lawn. It must have been deposited there by the flood. He crawled over to it and found it had a flat tire, but if he sat on it and pushed along with his left foot, he actually made some progress.

After about a block on the bike, he lost his concentration and toppled over. "I am pathetic," he said. But he got back up, and by noon he had reached the Spanish Fork McDonalds. He paused to sift through the dumpster and found some burnt apple pies that had probably been in there since before the flood, but he savored every bite.

He continued east and got on the old highway that led him straight into Springville. His pace was still slow, but after a few more hours he found himself turning the corner onto the Daltons' street.

When he reached the house, he was stunned to see the minivan gone except for a few parts piled on the lawn, and the Volkswagen was up on cinderblocks with the tires missing. The cars had been fine when he had brought the money just a few days before the flood, so it probably happened since the flood.

Tad looked around nervously, hoping the car thieves were long gone. He could only imagine what they would do to him if they knew he had $10,000.

Tad tossed the bike aside and cautiously entered the house. He listened for any noise, but the house was empty. He then quickly went to the cellar where he had hidden the money. If he hurried, he could probably get to the medical clinic before sunset. If everything went well and he started feeling better, then he could continue his journey to Hobble Creek Canyon.

However, when Tad tried to open the cellar door, it was being blocked somehow. He shoved it as hard as he could and finally got it partially open. To his dismay, the cellar was filled almost to the ceiling with mud. The cellar's lone window was next to the Daltons' garden, and the floodwaters had shattered the window. The swirling water had then rushed in and deposited most of the garden's top soil into the cellar. Tad's money was now buried under six feet of mud.

"Awwwgh!" Tad shouted. "I can't believe this."

He slumped against the wall. His energy was spent, and he had nowhere to turn. He finally decided to simply stay in the house and try to recover.

"I'm doing my best, Lord," he prayed, "but I'm going to need some help."

CHAPTER 20

Down in Guatemala, Josh was starting to feel isolated. He received several reports a day on his laptop about the problems in the United States, and he was aware that millions of Mexican citizens had fled northward, but he had no idea what was happening in southern Mexico along the path where he would soon lead the Quetzaltenango group. To calm his worries, he selected four of his most valiant missionaries and asked them to leave the valley as spies. He asked them to travel northward along the Pan-American Highway and return in one week.

It was a tense week for Josh as he worried whether he had sent the young men to their deaths, but they returned exactly one week later. Their report was sobering. In their journey, they hadn't seen a living soul, but they had come across recent battlefields with bodies spread across the land as far as they could see.

"It looked like a battle for survival, but no one survived," one of the missionaries said. "It reminded me of the descriptions of the Jaredites' final battle."

Soon afterward, Josh received an interesting message from the Church. It told about a young man in a mountain camp who had designed a way to make very sturdy handcarts out of golf carts. The name of the young man was familiar to him, so Josh looked closely at the photo that accompanied the message.

"Hey, Kim, come look at this," he called out. "David North has turned into an inventor. Good for him!"

The Browns had known that Becky and Doug had gone to a mountain camp, but they hadn't heard about whether the Norths had also gone, so it was a relief for them to see David's smiling photo next to his handcart.

"I was a little worried about Tad's spirituality when we saw him last," Josh said. "The whole 'Tadinator' thing was a little creepy. But if David is at the camp, I'm guessing the whole family is there."

That night Josh pondered David's handcart design and wondered how he could implement it into their group. Suddenly the name "Brother Mathoni" came into his mind. The man had been so eager to help out, but so far Josh hadn't utilized him at all.

The next morning Josh printed off David's design and went searching for Brother Mathoni. He found him helping a young family cook their breakfast.

"Brother Mathoni, do you have a minute?" Josh asked.

The man leaped right up from where he was scrambling some eggs. "Certainly, Elder Brown. It is wonderful to see you again. How can I help you?"

Josh handed him the printout of the handcart design. "The Church sent this to us, and when I saw it, I felt I needed to show it to you. It seems you have as much experience as anyone here. But as I was walking over here, I couldn't remember seeing any golf courses."

Brother Mathoni laughed. "No, golf isn't exactly a popular sport around here. I think there are a few courses for the tourists in Guatemala City, but we would have trouble finding any golf carts within a couple hundred miles."

"Hmm. Then maybe this plan won't work for us."

Brother Mathoni looked closely at the designs for a moment. "We don't have golf carts, but we have dozens of abandoned street carts in this city. I think this design would work well in converting them into something we could use on our journey."

Really?" Josh asked. "That would be great."

Brother Mathoni said, "Then with your permission, I would like to have several of the men help me gather up some carts from the city and we'll see what we can do."

Josh eagerly gave his consent, and over the next week Brother

Mathoni and a small army of helpers had gathered more than 100 carts from the city. When they had their first modified cart completed, Brother Mathoni pulled it to the temple to demonstrate how it worked to Josh.

"I'm impressed," Josh said as he gave the cart a try. "Build as many as you can before we leave."

Brother Mathoni said, "We will do our best. My goal is to have one for each family. It would make our journey so much easier."

"That would be wonderful," Josh told him. "You are a good man."

Under Brother Mathoni's direction, the men scoured the abandoned city once again and gathered anything that might be usable on the journey. They had also caught hundreds of chickens that provided both meat and eggs for the group.

Josh found himself more and more intrigued by Brother Mathoni. The man seemed to accomplish more than ten men could, and his organizational skills were unmatched. Yet he always deferred to Josh on any major decision. He often said to Josh, "You are the presiding priesthood leader in this area, but may I recommend that we . . ."

It was almost as if Brother Mathoni already knew in great detail what the group would face on its journey.

One night after another wonderful meeting with Brother Mathoni, Josh had a hard time sleeping because he felt so alive with the Spirit. Brother Mathoni's suggestions had been exactly what the group needed. Josh started to wonder if this man was the angel that Elder Smith had mentioned.

Finally he went to his office and opened the Book of Mormon, searching for a specific chapter. "Ah, there it is," he said, opening to Third Nephi 28. The chapter began:

"And it came to pass when Jesus had said these words, he spake unto his disciples, one by one, saying unto them: What is it that ye desire of me, after that I am gone to the Father?

"*And they all spake, save it were three, saying: We desire that after we have lived unto the age of man, that our ministry, wherein thou hast called us, may have an end, that we may speedily come unto thee in thy kingdom.*

"*And he said unto them: Blessed are ye because ye desired this thing of me; therefore, after that ye are seventy and two years old ye shall come unto me in my kingdom; and with me ye shall find rest.*

"*And when he had spoken unto them, he turned himself unto the three, and said unto them: What will ye that I should do unto you, when I am gone unto the Father?*

"*And they sorrowed in their hearts, for they durst not speak unto him the thing which they desired.*

"*And he said unto them: Behold, I know your thoughts, and ye have desired the thing which John, my beloved, who was with me in my ministry, before that I was lifted up by the Jews, desired of me.*

"*Therefore, more blessed are ye, for ye shall never taste of death; but ye shall live to behold all the doings of the Father unto the children of men, even until all things shall be fulfilled according to the will of the Father, when I shall come in my glory with the powers of heaven.*

"*And ye shall never endure the pains of death; but when I shall come in my glory ye shall be changed in the twinkling of an eye from mortality to immortality; and then shall ye be blessed in the kingdom of my Father.*

"*And again, ye shall not have pain while ye shall dwell in the flesh, neither sorrow save it be for the sins of the world; and all this will I do because of the thing which ye have desired of me, for ye have desired that ye might bring the souls of men unto me, while the world shall stand.*"

As he read further in the chapter, he came to verse 30. "*And they are as the angels of God, and if they shall pray unto the Father in the name of Jesus they can show themselves unto whatsoever man it seemeth them good.*"

"Could it possibly be true?" Josh asked himself. He rapidly shuffled back a few chapters, trying to satisfy a hunch. He stopped at Third Nephi 19:4 and read:

"And it came to pass that on the morrow, when the multitude was gathered together, behold, Nephi and his brother whom he had raised from the dead, whose name was Timothy, and also his son, whose name was Jonas, and also Mathoni, and Mathonihah, his brother, and Kumen, and Kumenonhi, and Jeremiah, and Shemnon, and Jonas, and Zedekiah, and Isaiah—now these were the names of the disciples whom Jesus had chosen—and it came to pass that they went forth and stood in the midst of the multitude."

Josh stared at the name in middle of the verse. There it was, as plain as day. *Mathoni!*

Could one of the Lord's Nephite disciples really be serving as his righthand man? It made sense. If Brother Mathoni was truly one of the Three Nephites, wouldn't he want to help his own people as they embarked on one of the great journeys of all time?

Josh felt like his whole body was on fire, and he took that as a confirmation that his hunch was correct. He chuckled and then said to himself, "He's not Brother Mathoni—he *is* Mathoni. How cool is that?"

Josh sought out Mathoni first thing in the morning and asked him to go for a walk with him. When they were in a secluded spot, Josh said, "I don't quite know how to say this, but I have figured out who you are. You're a translated being! Now I feel a little intimidated."

Mathoni simply said, "We are both servants of the Lord. That's all that matters."

Josh smiled. "But I feel you should be the one leading this group, not me."

Mathoni shook his head. "You are the presiding Church authority in this area. I am a disciple of Jesus Christ, but the Church organization I was part of when I was mortal is long gone. I hold the priesthood, but you are the Lord's legal representative."

Josh was still a bit overwhelmed. "Does anyone else know who you are?" he asked.

"Not anyone here at the temple," Mathoni said. "I'd prefer to keep it that way, but I am glad you now know."

"Then who else knows?" Josh asked.

"Well, I had a nice visit with Elder Smith when he came to visit you. We became acquainted soon after he became an apostle, and we worked on a couple of projects together. I met him at the airport in Guatemala City, and then I rode with him in the car on his way here. They dropped me off a couple of blocks away just before they arrived at the temple. Elder Smith requested that I stick around and give you a hand with the journey, so here I am."

"How come I never saw you until after the hurricane?" Josh asked.

Mathoni shrugged. "I spent that time among the outlying wards in the valley, telling them they needed to be prepared for any disasters. That kept me pretty busy."

"No wonder some of those wards seemed so prepared when we made the announcement," Josh marveled.

"That's what I specialize in," Mathoni said. "You know, giving a little advance warning as a way to—"

The visit between Josh and Mathoni was unexpectedly interrupted when a member of the temple presidency ran toward them. "Elder Brown, we have looked all over for you," the man said. "Your wife took a bad fall down one of the staircases in the temple. She hit her head on the marble floor at the bottom and isn't breathing."

As the three men rushed toward the temple, Kim had died and was looking down on her lifeless body. She felt a warm sensation of joy pass through her, and she looked around to see dozens of people dressed in white bustling around.

Kim reached out and touched the arm of one lady. "What has happened to me? One second I was walking down the stairs, and the next thing I know I'm standing here with you."

The lady looked a little confused, then she noticed Kim's body on the floor below. "Is that your body down there?"

"Yes, it is."

The lady laughed. "I'm sorry. The temple is an interesting place for someone to die, because there are already so many spirits here that sometimes we don't notice."

The lady went on her way, and suddenly someone with a familiar face and dark brown hair approached. Kim rushed to her. "Tina! Oh, how I've missed you!"

Kim's sister Tina had died when they were both teenagers, but now Tina stood before her as a beautiful full-grown adult spirit.

Tina smiled broadly. "I was just summoned from the Spirit World. You aren't supposed to cross over to Paradise for several years, but I didn't want to pass up this opportunity to see you."

They hugged happily, and then Tina added, "I'm so proud of both you and Josh. Our family members are watching over you. I recently was shown the great calling Josh has been given. I could hardly believe it."

"Me neither. Who would have believed he would be a mission president and a member of the Seventy? I'm so proud of him."

Tina looked briefly confused. "Not those callings. The next one." Then she put her hand over her mouth. "Oops. Forget I said anything."

Kim was now the one who was a little puzzled, but she quickly forgot Tina's comment about a future calling as she noticed Josh's parents, Daniel and Heather Brown, standing nearby. She was very surprised. The last thing she had heard about them, they had been gathered with the Saints at the San Diego Temple.

Kim said, "No, this can't be right. This means you are . . ."

Daniel smiled and hugged her warmly. "Yes, we are dead. But everything is wonderful here. Don't worry about us."

"What happened?" Kim asked.

"We were traveling to Utah to be with Becky and Doug when the Las Vegas earthquake hit. Our car was thrown off the road, and we died instantly. We didn't suffer. We have plenty of work to do here, and everything is all right. This was meant to be."

Heather took Kim's hand. "Please tell Josh what has happened to us, and we also want you to e-mail Becky. She was expecting us to arrive weeks ago, and she has no idea where we are. She has been very worried, and it will ease her mind."

"I will do that," Kim said.

Kim noticed two younger-looking spirits, a boy and a girl, standing behind Josh's parents. They seemed to be in a slightly different dimension, and they also seemed a little bothered to see her. Tina turned to them and said, "Don't worry. She's going back."

Tina's words caused the two spirits to smile happily. "Who are they?" Kim asked.

"They are your future children," Tina said. "But it isn't time for them to come yet. They will have the privilege of being born in New Jerusalem. They were just nervous you were here to stay and wouldn't be their mother."

Kim was delighted to discover that she would someday have children. She wanted to speak to them, but suddenly everyone could hear Josh's voice as if it were coming over a loudspeaker. They turned to look at Kim's body on the floor, and they could see Josh and Mathoni giving her a blessing.

Josh said, "Kim, by the power of the Holy Melchizedek Priesthood, I command you to return to your body and complete your earthly mission."

Tina said, "It's time for you to go."

Kim gave her sister one final hug, waved to the two young spirits, then felt herself being pulled back toward her body. Within a second she was back inside of it. Her head was throbbing, and she opened her eyes to see her Josh and Mathoni staring down at her.

"Whew, you're back," Josh said. "I thought we had lost you."

Kim rested quietly for a moment, feeling groggy. But soon she remembered her experience in the Spirit World.

"Josh, I have many things to tell you," she said. "But first we need to e-mail your sister. There's something you and Becky need to know."

CHAPTER 21

One morning a few days later, Mathoni excitedly approached Josh. "I know we are planning to leave soon, but I have been shown something very urgent that you and I must do for the Lord before the group leaves for New Jerusalem. We need to depart tonight, and we'll be back in a couple of days. I'll spend the day getting a bus ready."

"Where are we going?" Josh asked. "It seems like a bad time for us to leave the group for so long."

Mathoni put his hand on Josh's shoulder. "If we don't go, a major prophecy in the Book of Mormon will go unfulfilled."

Josh nodded. "That's a good enough reason for me. What are we doing?"

"You'll find out tonight," Mathoni said with a smile. "We'll leave at sunset, if that is all right. Don't forget your scriptures!"

As Josh spent the day in his office making final preparations for the journey, he kept glancing outside where he could see Mathoni removing seat after seat out of the nicest bus he had ever seen in Guatemala. He wondered where Mathoni had found it.

As the day wore on, Josh kind of felt bad for Mathoni. It was a hot day, and it certainly couldn't be easy unscrewing all of those seats from the floor. But he had to say to himself, "He's a translated being. I think he can handle it."

Josh explained to Kim that he and Mathoni were going to be gone for a couple of days. She felt a little nervous about him leaving. "Is it that important?" she asked.

"I really think it is."

She nodded. "Ever since I saw our children waiting for us in the Spirit World, I feel calm you'll survive anything."

"That's a good way to look at it," Josh said, giving her a kiss. "I love you." He nearly told her who Mathoni really was, but he felt the time still wasn't right.

As evening approached, Josh found Mathoni checking the bus engine and inflating the tires with a portable air pump.

Mathoni greeted him and said, "I took the liberty of filling the tank and throwing in a few extra cans of fuel. I hope that is all right."

"Sheesh, how far are we going?" Josh asked.

"Well, the extra gas is partly because we're going to have a heavy load. By the way, I also grabbed 30 blankets."

Josh just shrugged. "Whatever you need is fine with me. But when can I find out where we are going?"

"As soon as we are on the road," Mathoni said. "If you don't mind, I'll drive."

"Be my guest," Josh said. "It seems like a guy like you would find driving boring, though."

"Never," Mathoni said. "It is one of my favorite hobbies. It started with the Model T Ford," Mathoni said, "but it sure is hard to beat driving a nice Porsche."

Josh laughed. "You really are an interesting guy."

"Hey, you have to realize that when I was translated I was shown a vision of the last days, and I saw all of these interesting vehicles zooming everywhere. So it wasn't exactly fun waiting 1,900 years for people to invent something faster than a chariot."

A few minutes later, Mathoni said, "I think we are far enough along on our journey that we can discuss where we are headed. Please open your scriptures and read Mormon 6:6 to me."

Josh flipped to the right page and read, "*And it came to pass that when we had gathered in all our people in one to the land of Cumorah, behold I, Mormon, began to be old; and knowing it to be the last struggle of my people, and having been commanded of the Lord that I should not suffer the records which had been handed down by our fathers, which were sacred, to fall into the hands of the Lamanites, (for the Lamanites would destroy them) therefore I made this record out of the plates of Nephi, and hid up in the hill Cumorah all the records which had been entrusted to me by the hand of the Lord, save it were these few plates which I gave unto my son Moroni."*

Josh looked away from the book. "Are we retrieving the plates?"

Mathoni grinned. "Yes, we are. The time has finally come to retrieve the plates that Mormon stored away and take them where they can be translated and shared with the Saints."

"But are we driving all the way to New York to the hill Cumorah?"

Mathoni laughed. "Hardly. The hill Cumorah that Mormon is talking about is within a couple hundred miles of here."

"Then how come the one in New York is called Cumorah?"

Mathoni thought for a moment. "I guess it is like when the Pilgrims came to America. They named a lot of their new villages after European cities they had come from. That's basically what Moroni did when he buried his set of plates in New York."

"Wow, I guess that makes sense."

Josh looked back at the empty bus. "So we are going to load those plates onto this bus and take them to New Jerusalem?"

"You are correct," Mathoni said. "The prophet is the one who holds the keys of translation, and when we get them to New Jerusalem, he will be able to translate them. The other apostles are also ordained as seers and revelators, and they will be able to help with the work if the prophet authorizes them to do so."

"Don't you already know the language?" Josh asked. "Couldn't you just do the translation work for us?"

Mathoni shrugged, "Yes, but I'm not authorized to . . ."

Josh held up his hands. "I get it. The work must be done by mortals."

✤ ✤ ✤

After they had been on the road for several hours on a quiet stretch of highway, Josh turned to Mathoni. "How much longer before we get there?"

"Probably another two hours," Mathoni said.

"Then I really need to take a restroom break," Josh said, dancing a little in his seat.

Mathoni laughed. "You need to keep reminding me of that, okay? It might have been days before I even thought of it."

Mathoni pulled the bus to the side of the road, and Josh darted into a grove of trees. As he was about to return to the bus, he heard someone call out to him, "Josh, I have a message for you."

Josh's head snapped around to see a man dressed in a white robe standing among the trees. He looked familiar, so Josh walked back toward him. "Have we met before?" Josh asked.

"We most certainly have," the man said with a smile. "I am a messenger from the other side of the veil, and I've been watching the great work you are doing among the people in Quetzaltenango."

"Thank you," Josh said. "The Lord has blessed us."

The man nodded. "Yes, he has, and that is why you need to keep the people where they are. The time has been delayed indefinitely for you to lead them to New Jerusalem."

That news didn't feel right to Josh, and he looked curiously at the man. "I didn't catch your name . . ."

"My name doesn't matter," the man said, his face clouding with anger. He leapt at Josh and pushed him to the ground. Josh felt a heavy darkness settle over him. The man was seemingly choking the life right out of him!

"Heavenly Father, help me," Josh whispered, and the man became even more enraged, tightening his grip around Josh's neck. Just as Josh was about to lose consciousness, he felt someone slam into the man, knocking him to the ground and freeing Josh.

Josh turned to watch Mathoni and the man in white battle in hand-to-hand combat. They wrestled viciously, and the man in the white robe clung to Mathoni like glue. They battled each other for several seconds, and in the process the man's white robe turned a dark color. During the struggle, Mathoni shouted to Josh, "Run back to the bus! I'll keep Satan busy until you get there."

Josh's mouth fell open. *Satan?*

Satan broke free from Mathoni, then called out to Josh, "Don't listen to this fool! I only want great things for you. I could make you a powerful ruler in my kingdom!"

Josh seemed rooted to the ground, stunned to have the Great Deceiver standing before him. "Why would I want to be in your kingdom?" Josh asked. "You tried to kill me."

"I was merely testing you," Satan said. "You did well. I would never want you to die."

Mathoni stepped toward him and angrily said, "There you go again with your lies! Josh has more important things to do than join your crumbling kingdom."

Satan's eyes grew narrow. "You sure are confident, aren't you? My forces are growing stronger every day. At this rate we will easily prevail."

Mathoni shook his head. "You are mistaken, as usual, but nobody has ever been able to change your mind. Josh, let's get back to the bus."

Satan glared at them, then gathered his robe around him. As he moved toward the trees, he gave one final offer to Josh. "If things ever get too tough, just call on me. I can make your burdens light and give you anything you desire."

⚜ ⚜ ⚜

Josh was physically weakened by Satan's attack, and Mathoni had to carry him to the bus. Josh slept for two hours as they crossed into southern Mexico, pausing occasionally so Mathoni could step outside and throw some boulders or an abandoned car off the road.

When Josh was feeling a little stronger, he ate some vegetables Mathoni had packed for him. Then he said, "I've never felt such darkness. It felt like he was going to crush the life out of me."

Mathoni responded, "That's exactly what Satan wanted to do. He would kill every priesthood holder if he could, or at least turn them to his side. Satan is getting desperate, but he is both brilliant and stupid. He is foolish enough to think he can somehow win this war, and he is proud of the great spiritual destruction he and his followers are causing throughout the world."

"He does seem to be making a dent," Josh said.

"In some ways," Mathoni said. "But the people he really wants to destroy are the Saints and their leaders. He isn't doing so well at capturing his greatest targets, and it makes him furious. He particularly hates General Authorities, and now you're a target more than ever. He knows the odds are slim that you would ever turn to him, but he never gives up. Of course, he has always hated you in particular."

"But why would he care so much about me?" Josh asked. "I guess I should consider it some sort of honor, but doesn't he have bigger fish to fry than me?"

Mathoni was quiet for several seconds. "Josh, a person shouldn't know too much about their own future, but as you know, I have been privileged to see in vision how this story ends. This won't be the last time Satan tries to destroy you, so always be on your guard."

Josh felt a chill go down his spine. "What do you mean by the end of the story? The end of the world?"

Mathoni was silent again for a time, and he seemed to be praying. He finally said, "There are certain things I cannot tell you, but keep in mind that Satan remembers you from the premortal world, and he knows what you have been foreordained to do."

Josh was baffled. "That's a bit cryptic. Can't you tell me anything else?"

"No, that will do. The Lord trusts you a great deal, so don't disappoint him," Mathoni said. "I'll leave it at that."

⚜ ⚜ ⚜

As the sun began to rise, they approached a tall mountain. The bus moved slowly along a narrow mountain road, inching its way toward a peak that could be seen in the distance.

"I'm guessing you've been here before," Josh said.

"Several times," Mathoni answered. "I even helped choose the site. When Ammoron asked for guidance in where to store the plates, my brethren and I recommended this peak. We knew this mountain wasn't volcanic, so it was chosen. There was once a temple on this mountain, and so it was convenient for Mormon when he was abridging the plates to retrieve the ones he needed from where they were stored and work on them in the temple."

"What happened to the temple?"

"It was destroyed by the Lamanites, just like everything else they could get their hands on that testified of Christ. Then the jungle just started reclaiming the mountain, and nobody even returned to this area for centuries."

"Then who built this road?" Josh asked.

"About 10 years ago I knew the time to retrieve the plates was fast approaching," Mathoni said. "So I encouraged some of the men from the valley to build this road as a shortcut to a neighboring village. It helped them find new customers for their fruits and vegetables, and it also opened the way for us to retrieve the plates."

"Can you tell me about the prophet Moroni?" Josh asked.

"Well, I spent a lot of time with him during his travels across North America on his way to New York. I admire him greatly. He would get pretty lonely, so I would walk along with him and help carry the plates sometimes. They could get pretty heavy for him."

Mathoni slowed the bus and scanned the hillside before saying, "Speaking of the plates, we're here!"

They climbed out of the bus, and Mathoni pointed to a 20-foot-high cliff. There were a few boulders at its base. "We're going to need to build a ramp to get the plates out," he said. "The cave was once at ground level, but the canyon has eroded away. See the large boulder that is jutting out? It is covering the cave entrance."

Over the next hour, Mathoni directed Josh in cutting down some small trees, and Mathoni quickly created an effective wooden ramp three feet wide that reached up to the boulder and sloped gently to the trail.

Once the ramp was stable, both men worked their way up to the boulder. Mathoni said, "This cave can only be opened by a mortal who has been given the authority to do so. You have been given that authority, correct?"

"Yes, Elder Smith of the Quorum of the Twelve told me I was authorized to perform any necessary Church action in this area, although this isn't exactly what I had in mind."

Josh pushed on the boulder, but it was wedged in tightly. "How did Mormon and Moroni get this closed?" he asked.

"It was a lot easier to roll it into place," Mathoni said. He handed Josh a small log to use as a lever, and slowly the boulder began to move. Josh wiggled the log deeper along one of the edges, and finally it popped loose. It tumbled past the ramp and then crashed loudly down the slope and into the forest.

Josh peered into the cave, unsure of what he would see. Mathoni handed him a flashlight, and Josh shined the light inside. To his delight, he saw a narrow room about 10-feet high and 15-feet square. Along each of the four walls were wooden shelves reaching to the ceiling, and each shelf was stacked high with glittering metal plates.

Josh said jokingly, "We're rich!"

Mathoni frowned. "Be careful. That phrase doesn't go over well with the protecting angels. I wouldn't say it again unless you want to get zapped."

Josh gulped and looked around. "Sorry, angels," he said. "I was only kidding!"

Mathoni climbed down the ramp and backed up the bus. He opened the back door of the bus and placed the end of the ramp inside it. Then over the next few minutes they created a pulley system with some rope and a plastic crate that Mathoni had brought along. They decided that Josh would put a set of plates into the crate and then lower it down the ramp to Mathoni, who would then put the plates in the bus while Josh pulled the crate back up and reloaded it. Within two hours they had moved approximately 200 sets of plates from the cave into the bus.

Josh's arms were exhausted. Each set of plates weighed between 50 and 80 pounds, and he figured they had moved about 10,000 pounds of plates. Mathoni had carefully distributed the plates throughout the bus, but it was still a full load.

When the last set of plates was in the bus, Mathoni walked up the ramp and stood inside the cave with Josh. A warm feeling enveloped them. "This is a sacred place," Josh said. "I feel privileged to have seen it."

"Just compare how you feel right now to how you felt when Satan was choking you. It should be clear which side of the battle you want to be on."

Josh's chest was nearly bursting with emotion. "I know."

✤ ✤ ✤

They quickly covered the plates with the blankets Mathoni had brought. Then Mathoni pointed to a set of plates he had placed in the passenger's seat. "I know you can't read them, but I thought you might enjoy holding them for a few minutes. They were very special to my family."

"What are they?" Josh asked.

"The brass plates." Mathoni said, getting a little choked up. "Why don't you set them aside for a moment and open your scriptures to Alma 37:3-4. It will be a good way to end our day by reading about their importance."

Josh found the verses in his Book of Mormon and read, "*And these plates of brass, which contain these engravings, which have the records of the holy scriptures upon them, which have the genealogy of our forefathers, even from the beginning—*

"*Behold, it has been prophesied by our fathers, that they should be kept and handed down from one generation to another, and be kept and preserved by the hand of the Lord until they should go forth unto every kindred, tongue, and people, that they shall know of the mysteries contained thereon."*

"Wow, we are fulfilling this prophecy today," Josh said.

"Yes, and I wanted to keep these plates separate from the others because I think the prophet will want to translate them first when we get to New Jerusalem."

Mathoni then settled into the driver's seat. "How about if I keep on driving?" he asked.

"I think that's a great idea, " Josh said. "The last thing I need is some future scripture to read, '*And thus did Elder Brown drive the precious cargo of plates off the side of the mountain.*"

Mathoni smiled. "That would definitely complicate things."

Late the following night Mathoni pulled the bus into the Quetzaltenango Temple parking lot.

"I suggest we keep the contents of this bus as our little secret," Mathoni said. "Even Kim doesn't need to know. These Saints are good people, but there's no reason to tempt them."

Josh agreed, and Mathoni parked next to a shed that was filled with rice and beans. "We need to cover the plates with something that can't be uncovered easily, and I thought this bus could be disguised as our main food transporter. It will help explain why we are taking a bus along on the journey when everyone else will be walking or pushing a cart."

"That makes sense to me," Josh said. "Joseph Smith once hid the gold plates in a barrel of beans when he was traveling, so I guess this comes close to that, just on a much grander scale."

"I like that comparison," Mathoni said. Then he slapped Josh on the back. "I can get the bus loaded with the food tonight while everyone is still sleeping, and then the plates will be safe. Good job, Josh. I know it has been a long trip for you, so go get some sleep."

The two servants of the Lord shook hands, then Josh went to his room. He desperately wanted to tell Kim all the things he had experienced, but the time to tell her still had not come.

CHAPTER 22

The very day that Josh and Mathoni retrieved the plates, the Jolley's Ranch leaders received a message on President Johnson's laptop that their group had been selected to join a larger group that was gathering at the Manti Temple. The Church leaders wanted the group to be in Manti as soon as possible.

The camp's leaders had known all along that this camp was temporary, and was designed more to weed out everyone who wasn't ready to live a consecrated lifestyle. That task of "sifting" had been accomplished during the summer months, and the Saints who remained at the Jolley's Ranch camp were among the finest people on earth. They were fully capable of the great mission that awaited them.

President Johnson immediately made the announcement to the camp, and everyone was excited to travel to Manti. It would be wonderful to be near a temple once again. The rest of the day was spent busily loading up items in the handcarts. The plan was to leave right after breakfast and work their way through the back canyons to Manti.

Emma slept restlessly in her cot that night. She had been able to keep her mind off Tad most of the time, but on this night she couldn't stop thinking about him. Despite his poor choices, she still loved him and felt an eternal bond with him. But she knew that if the camp moved, she might never see him again in this life.

When she finally dozed off, a peculiar dream filled her mind. She found herself in a glorious room filled with light, and she somehow sensed she was remembering an event she had participated in before her birth. She and other family members were watching her future husband be foreordained to serve as a bishop during his earth life. After the ordination, Tad had given her a hug. He told her with a smile, "I can't wait to get to earth and serve the Lord!"

Emma awoke with a start. The dream was both amazing and frustrating. The odds were very slim of her husband ever becoming a bishop now. Emma worried whether Tad had even survived the destruction in the valley.

Emma suddenly noticed a bright light at the end of her cot. Grandpa North stood there in spirit form, wearing a holy robe. He looked youthful and full of strength, unlike the frail, cancer-ridden body he had suffered with during his last days on earth.

"Don't give up on Tad," he told Emma.

"What do you mean?" she asked. "Tad made the choice to stay behind. He threw everything away."

Grandpa North nodded. "Yes, he made serious errors, but he is repenting of them. His heart is still pure, and he has asked for the Lord's help. He is hiding at your parents' home in Springville, hoping for a miracle. He has nowhere to turn. Go find him. With your help, he can still fulfill his mission in life."

Before Emma could even respond, Grandpa North faded away. Emma's mind was racing. First there was the vivid dream of the premortal world, followed by a heavenly visit. Or was that just a dream too? "No, that was real," Emma told herself, still sensing a holy aura in the air.

She got up and went to Doug's tent. She quietly pulled him out of bed and led him to a nearby kitchen where they could talk. She told him what she had just experienced, but he was skeptical. "Dad and I were down at the house just a few days ago and the place was empty. Do you really think he is there now?"

Emma shrugged. "Grandpa North just came to me from the Spirit World and said Tad is at the house. Don't you think we better trust him?"

"You're right," Doug said. "It seems like family members on the other side are more understanding about Tad's actions than we have been. If you want, I'll go find him."

"No, Grandpa North made it sound like it needed to be me," Emma said. "Besides, you need to stay here to get the camp ready for the move."

"It's just that I'm a little worried for you," Doug said. "It's dangerous down there. Barry Newton wasn't chasing me down to catch up on old times—he wanted to literally catch me!"

"I'll be fine," Emma said. "My main worry is how I'll respond when I see Tad. Until about ten minutes ago, all I've wanted to do is choke him for the way he abandoned us."

Doug chuckled. "Go easy on him, even if he deserves to be roughed up a little."

"I just don't understand," Emma said. "How did things turn out this way? Tad was a good man. His patriarchal blessing even talks about him being a bishop someday."

"I actually was thinking about that the other night," Doug said. He picked up a deck of Uno cards from a table. "Sometimes our lives are like this card game. On every turn you have different options. You can either match the color or match the number, and every card you put down affects the rest of the game. For some reason Tad put down the wrong card a few months back, and now you are his only chance to get his game back on track."

The first hint of dawn had reached the camp, and so they quickly put together a backpack of food and water for Emma to take with her. Within ten minutes she was ready to go, but she fretted about leaving the children.

"You worry about finding your husband," Doug said. "We can handle the kids."

Doug gave her a ride on the ATV down past the golf course to the paved canyon trail. "I'd let you take the ATV, but we are sending out a scout team ahead of us and they need it," he said.

"I understand," she said. "But where should I meet you? Once I find Tad, you'll be way ahead of us."

"Just head to Manti," Doug said. "Don't stay in the valley any longer than needed. We'll be praying for you."

They hugged good-bye, then she slipped through the opening in the fence and started walking down the canyon's paved bike path. As she exited the canyon an hour later and moved into Springville, she saw first-hand the devastation the earthquakes and flood had caused. The biggest effect was a general feeling of decay, accompanied by a stench of sogginess and mold.

As she approached Center Street, she saw movement in one of the houses. She immediately sprinted away. After a block or so, she looked back to see a man standing on the sidewalk watching her.

"Heavenly Father, please protect me," she prayed. "Grandpa North said Tad would be here. Please guide me to him."

She would be at her parents' house within ten minutes, and despite Tad's faults, she was more eager to see her husband again than she had thought possible.

⁕ ⁕ ⁕

Tad sat alone and depressed in a dark corner of the living room. He had just finished eating a bottle of cherries that he had salvaged from the cellar. He had given up on ever digging deep enough to find the $10,000, but he did uncover several bottles of cherries that had swirled to the top of the mud before it solidified.

Unfortunately, the fruit had caused havoc to Tad's digestive system, but he knew he had to keep eating whatever he could find to keep up his strength. He had lost track of time, but he figured he had been there for four days.

He took the empty cherry bottle and limped back to the cellar, where he used the bottle as a shovel to dig through the mud once again for any food that might still be there. As he tossed aside another scoop of dirt, he heard a door creak upstairs.

Tad looked frantically around for the baseball bat he had used to chase off some men the day before. Then he heard someone call out, "Tad? Hello? Are you here?"

Tad crept quietly out of the cellar and cautiously glanced into the living room. A woman was standing in the doorway. He shook his head, not believing his eyes. "Is that you, Emma?"

The woman smiled. "Yes, it's me."

They rushed into each other's arms, and Emma quickly held her breath. She loved her husband, but he really stunk.

"Oh, Emma, I have missed you so much," Tad said. "How are the kids? Is everyone okay?"

"Everyone is doing fine. They're all just worried about you." Then she noticed the bloody wrapping on his right hand. "What happened to you?"

"That's where my chip was," Tad said. "I cut it out myself."

"Let me look at it." Emma carefully loosened the wrapping so she could see the wound. "Ouch! That looks really bad. Did you use a knife?"

"No, a broken bottle. All I can say is it was harder to get the chip out than it was to put it in."

Tad then pointed to his foot, which was still swollen to twice its normal size. "A boulder fell on it during the earthquake, and it only seems to be getting worse. I was going to come find you in the canyon, but this was as far as I could go."

Emma looked at her injured, dirt-covered husband who reeked of cherries, and for the first time in a long time, she felt compassion for him. "It looks like you've been through a lot."

Tad wiped his eyes. "I was such a fool to listen to my boss. I can see now that the chip is part of a plan to turn people from the Lord. In order to keep my job, they demanded I make an oath saying I wasn't a member of the Church anymore, and I just couldn't do it. They were probably going to put me in jail, but I escaped. That's when I cut the chip out of my hand, and I've been hiding ever since. There is one government agent who I'm sure would kill me if he found me."

Emma listened sympathetically, but she also felt he had created his own problems. "You've had a rough time, but didn't you know this was how it was going to end up? We had talked about this for months! We had agreed to never get the chip."

"You have to realize that my intentions weren't all bad," Tad said. "I was just being cautious in case . . ."

"In case of what?" Emma interrupted. "In case the prophet and apostles were wrong? The kids and I have eaten three meals a day ever since we joined the camp, while you've apparently been living off my mom's bottled cherries. What was the better choice?"

Tad broke down in tears. "You were absolutely right. I admit I had my doubts because we have been warned to be prepared for so long and nothing seemed to happen, then the bottom fell out in just a few months."

"It's called showing a little faith," Emma said, feeling torn. She was excited to see her husband, but she was also still angry at him and his foolish decisions. She desperately hoped he had really changed, but if he hadn't, he might cause problems if she allowed him to join the group.

"Can you tell me some ways you are different now?" Emma asked. "How are you doing with your obsessions about the Gladiatorzz or having a big salary?"

"Well, neither one has brought me much to cheer about lately," he said, trying to lighten the mood.

"Exactly. What I'm asking is if I am going to get back the husband I once had—the man who honored his priesthood and was an example to his children," Emma said. "To be honest, I felt like we've been holding to the Iron Rod together for all these years, and then suddenly you let go and took off running toward the Great and Spacious Building. I was forced to choose between staying with our children on the right path, or joining you. Sorry to say, it wasn't a hard decision. I chose to keep holding onto the rod—even if it meant I lost my husband."

Tad completely understood what she was saying. He knew he had not been a good husband or father for quite a while. "Well, I have no excuse for the past few months, but I do feel I am back on track. I want to feel worthy again."

He limped over to the couch and grabbed a water-damaged set of scriptures. "The past few days I've read most of the Doctrine and

Covenants. The prophecies are all coming true! As I read them, I knew I needed to get back on the Lord's side. I asked Him for a second chance. I think your arrival means He has granted it. How did you know where I was?"

"You have your Grandpa North to thank for that," she said. She then told him of the vision she had received.

Tad was overcome with emotion. "Maybe there still is hope for me," he said.

"I think so," she said. She opened up the backpack of food and tossed him a bag of beef jerky. His eyes lit up as he tore open the bag and he shoved a strip of jerky in his mouth.

"Ahh, I love you," he said, and tried to pull her close, but she pushed him away.

"I love you too," she said, "but that combination of jerky and cherries on your breath is making me sick."

They discovered there was still some cold water available in the taps. At Emma's suggestion, Tad took a freezing bath and used some mouthwash that was in the cupboard. They also checked his foot again, and while they could tell there was something seriously wrong with it, Emma didn't want to hurt it further. She felt they should just get back to the group and have a doctor look at it.

"Then let's go join the group," Tad said. "I'm tired of this place."

"That's the problem," Emma said. "The group left this morning and is gathering with other groups at the Manti Temple. They are working their way there through the back canyons, rather than risk coming into the valley and being attacked. Doug told me that I should just head for Manti if I found you."

It was getting late in the day, and they didn't want to get caught outside in the dark, so they decided to leave first thing in the morning and travel to Spanish Fork Canyon, where they hoped to meet up with the Jolley's Ranch group.

Emma wanted to sleep on the couch, but Tad felt they needed to stay in the cellar. "It is the only safe place," Tad said. "Nearly every night someone has come through the house."

That news frightened Emma, and they made a makeshift bed in the cellar out of couch cushions on top of the mud. Tad had blocked off the cellar's broken window, and it was actually warm inside. They stayed cuddled together throughout the night, and despite their recent marital difficulties, they were truly happy to be in each other's arms again. Emma told Tad about the Jolley's Ranch camp, and how their son David had turned into a man over the summer, helping with many projects and the recognition he had been given for his handcart idea.

"I should have been there," Tad said sadly. "I can't wait to see the kids again. I'm so tired of feeling unsafe."

The wind began to howl at around midnight, and it helped keep any prowlers away. But to their surprise they awoke to an inch of snow on the ground, which was not typical for early October.

Emma searched through her parents' attic and found a couple of warm coats and gloves. She also discovered a pair of old "moon boots" that Tad could wear to soften the pain on his injured foot.

"I think those boots were Doug's when he was a Boy Scout," Emma said with a laugh. "I'm glad my mom never got rid of them."

Tad squirmed a little. "Speaking of Doug, I'm a little worried to see him and your dad again."

"What do you mean?" Emma asked,

"Maybe they won't accept me back. After my last encounter with them at our apartment, they still might be happier to never see me again."

"Don't worry. I think they'll be ready to forgive and forget."

Throughout the day, Doug's mind had been on his sister. He hoped Tad had been at the house and could be with Emma as she traveled to rejoin them. He hated to imagine her out there alone.

The group had made steady progress along the mountain roads, and Doug had hoped to reach Spanish Fork Canyon within two or three days. But the unexpected snow had slowed them down, and they had also been forced to spend some time removing large rocks from the road that had fallen during the latest earthquake. However, the group's spirits remained high, and they eagerly looked forward to reaching Manti.

As the Jolley's Ranch group journeyed through the mountains, the United States was at its weakest point since the Revolutionary War. The country had been downtrodden then, but at that time the nation's leaders had turned to the Lord for protection, and He had answered their prayers in miraculous ways.

Unfortunately, this time there wasn't a righteous leader such as George Washington to rally the citizens. In fact, the U.S. president and Congressional leaders had essentially stopped listening to the people they governed. They particularly avoided meeting with anyone who had a religious motive.

The media had successfully labeled all Christians as fanatics, and the nation's laws had been relaxed to the point that essentially nothing was morally wrong anymore—except such things as prayer in school or mentioning Jesus Christ in a public setting. However, pornographic images were welcomed on billboards and in magazines. America was drenched in sexual filth, and it was like a great plague that was oozing across the nation.

Marriages rarely took place anymore, because consenting adults were now legally able to do whatever they pleased. Also, if you happened to have a companion who was the same gender as you, bravo to you! America wished you the best in your relationship.

In other words, the nation had turned its back on the Lord's commandments. It couldn't have happened at a worse possible moment.

CHAPTER 23

The lessons of world history were about to turn the tables on the United States with a vengeance. Other countries that felt downtrodden or abused by the United States had quietly prepared for a time when they could crush the American way of life. All they were waiting for was a chink in America's armor.

In the late 1980s, the Soviet Union had collapsed under its own weight, ending what had been known as the Cold War. As U.S. President Ronald Reagan steadily pushed for democracy in that region, the Soviet Union's so-called "Evil Empire" had soon splintered into several nations.

The Berlin Wall was torn down, symbolizing the advancement of democratic forms of government. Various forms of democracy were attempted in these nations, and for a time it appeared that freedom would flourish.

But as the new century began and the world turned its eyes to the troubles in the Middle East, the fallen Russian giant began to rebuild itself. They focused on developing their oil refineries, and after a few years, money was no longer a problem. Meanwhile, their hatred of America had only deepened.

The philosophies of former Russian leaders Lenin and Stalin were still alive in the hearts of many of their leaders, and they carefully strengthened their military. As early as 2007 it had been clear to U.S. military experts that Russia's new nuclear missiles were more powerful than they had ever been, and that the U.S. would be helpless to stop them.

To the south of Russia lay China, another country that

had enormous military firepower, as well as more than a billion citizens. Their relationship with the United States had been somewhat peaceful for many decades, but the Chinese leaders were growing perturbed by the widening trade imbalance between the two countries. China's businesses were producing and shipping billions of dollars of products to the United States each year, while American companies were hardly doing likewise.

This situation was fine as long as the Americans paid their bills, but Chinese leaders were beginning to feel nervous. There were signs pointing to an eventual collapse of the U.S. economy, and that would create economic trouble for China as well.

These conditions were magnified by the U.S. involvement in the Middle East. In many respects, Russia and China didn't want democracy to take root there, and so they quietly gave aid to the extremist groups in Iran, Afghanistan, and Syria, prolonging the conflicts and sapping America's military strength.

This situation may have continued for several years, but then the Chinese president had an idea. He asked Russia's leader to visit him at his palace. Over the course of two days, the history of the world was forever altered. The previous leaders of these countries had always envisioned destroying America. But a new idea had been hatched. They asked themselves, "Rather than destroying America, why not occupy it?"

The leaders congratulated each other on their plan. North America was a fertile, spacious continent, and they could certainly divide it fairly. China certainly could see the advantages of expansion, and Russia still held a grudge over the Cold War.

They had also cultivated the support of several Islamic countries who would love to assist them. It would be fairly easy to persuade those countries to stop sending oil to America based on hatred alone, but they would be promised great wealth for their help.

And thus was formed the Coalition, a group of countries with the goal to overthrow the United States and eventually claim it as their own. Their secret plans had taken several years to organize, such as coordinating their military forces, but with the United

States currently in an unsettled turmoil, the time had finally come to put their plans into effect.

The next morning, as Tad and Emma were about to leave for Manti, he couldn't help thinking about the $10,000. Maybe the money's main purpose had been to get him out of Salt Lake, but Tad now felt there was another reason he had withdrawn the money. He told Emma he felt they needed to dig it up.

"But why would we need it now?" she asked.

"I really feel I need to give it to the Church. I haven't paid tithing since you left, and the $10,000 would more than cover what I owed. I just feel I need to do it as part of my repentance process, and I certainly could use the blessings."

Emma got a little emotional. "That is wonderful. I'm proud of you for even thinking of it."

"Thank you. I'll bet if we worked together we could recover it within a couple of hours."

They used the empty cherry bottles to scoop out the mud. As the hole got deeper, Emma kept digging, since she was in better physical shape than Tad. She would scoop out the mud and give the bottle to Tad, who would dump it in a pile and hand her the previous one. They actually made good time.

As they neared the floor of the cellar, Tad said, "I'm glad I can use the money to pay my tithing, but I just feel bad that I never got to use it like I wanted. My plan was to use the money to make a down-payment on a house for you here in Springville."

Emma laughed. "Well, I do appreciate the thought, but I've got my pick of houses now. They all have a lot of mold in them, but they won't cost us a dime!"

Within minutes Emma removed the concrete covering and pulled the briefcase from the hole. Tad popped it open and was relieved to see the briefcase's seal had kept the bills dry.

Emma's eyes widened. "Wow, that's a lot of $20 bills."

They decided they didn't want to carry the briefcase all the way to Manti, so Emma found some Zip-Lock plastic bags in a drawer and they put the money in the bags. Then they put the bags in a backpack for Tad to wear.

They took a few minutes to eat more of the supplies Emma had brought, then they began their journey to Spanish Fork Canyon. They reached 400 East and stayed right in the middle of the road. They felt vulnerable, but the overnight snowfall and cold weather seemed to work in their favor, keeping any potential attackers off the streets.

Tad's foot began to give him problems after just a few blocks. Emma found him a sturdy stick to use as a crutch, but their pace slowed to about one block every 15 minutes. By the time they reached the point where 400 East merged with Highway 89 heading into Mapleton, it was clear they weren't going to make it to Spanish Fork Canyon that day. They needed to find a place to stay during the night where they would be undisturbed. A patch of trees was visible just a few blocks ahead—the Springville Evergreen Cemetery.

"That looks like a good place to stay," Emma said. "I doubt anyone will bother us there."

Tad wasn't overly pleased with the idea. "What about ghosts?" he asked, only half-joking. "It might be spooky."

"I'm more worried about the living creatures around here than the dead ones," she said with a roll of her eyes. "Don't worry, I'll protect you."

They entered through the cemetery gates, and the grass was several inches high. It was clear the maintenance crew was no longer on the job. Emma led Tad into the western part of the cemetery, where they had a clear view of the valley. Emma found the headstone of her grandparents, Keith and Rosalie Dalton, and she cleaned up around the stone and pulled some weeds.

"I know the grass will grow back, but I just want it to look nice," she said.

Then they moved toward some nearby trees where there was a small headstone with a lamb carved into the top of it. Emma smiled to herself. As a teenager, Emma had attended a neighbor's graveside service and then she had tripped on the grass and hit her head on that little lamb.

They spent a very cold night in that grove of trees, huddled against a large headstone to shield themselves from the wind. The next morning they both felt too ill and weak to travel further, and they decided to rest for one more day.

Emma didn't think Doug's group could have made it very far in the snow anyway. She figured they would still have time to catch up to the group in the next couple of days.

In many respects, being ill that day was a blessing for them. Since they had no contact with the rest of the country, they weren't aware that spending that fateful day hidden in a Utah cemetery was the best thing they could have done.

⁘ ⁘ ⁘

Tad's former boss Ken was walking to his office in the City Creek Center that day when he saw a crowd of people watching a TV in a nearby donut shop. He saw the words "Oil Freeze" across the bottom of the screen.

"What's going on?" Ken asked a lady standing nearby.

"The countries in the Middle East aren't going to send us any more oil," the lady said in a worried voice.

Ken couldn't believe his ears. He rushed to his office and pulled up the story on an internet news site. It was true. The oil-producing countries in the Middle East had voted unanimously to stop sending oil to the United States. Even Saudi Arabia had joined them. These countries had made threats in the past, but this time it looked like they were serious.

All Ken could do was stare at the computer screen. He knew his company was doomed, and his life was basically ruined.

Within hours, the price of gasoline began to climb drastically, and a day later the first economic fallout began when the major airlines announced "temporary suspensions" of all flights because of fuel costs. Within a few days those cutbacks became permanent.

Those cancellations were followed by bankruptcy announcements by the airlines. No one seemed to care about the airlines, because who could afford to fly now anyway?

Seemingly everyone who owned a car rushed to the nearest gas station to get any remaining fuel. Some lines stretched for 10 blocks, even though it was clear that the gas supply would run out long before the cars at the end of the line could be filled.

Within a week of the announcement, the United States went from being a bustling nation with crowded freeways and airports to one where people didn't leave their own community. Even if you had gas in your car, it just cost too much to go anywhere.

The U.S. president assured the nation that everything possible was being done to resume the oil shipments, but he didn't realize the oil-supplying nations had no intention of resuming their shipments. Their plan to cripple the United States had worked even better than they had expected, and the great American giant was suddenly very vulnerable.

The first outward signs of a national collapse came with the reports of riots and even gang warfare sprouting up throughout the nation. In Washington, D.C., mobs rallied in front of the Capitol Building and the White House, blaming the federal government for the situation. Thankfully the Saints in the area had already gathered to the grounds of the Washington D.C. Temple and were quietly staying clear of the growing dissension.

Violent protests were organized throughout the nation, where citizens demanded that the country begin drilling for oil immediately, but it was an unrealistic hope. Nearly all of the oil wells in the U.S. had either been damaged by the recent hurricanes or weren't in operation. It would take weeks before an adequate supply could be created.

Besides, due to environmental regulations, new oil refineries hadn't been built in the U.S. for decades. So even if the oil wells began production again, there weren't enough refineries to adequately process it.

As the country's difficulties escalated, Washington D.C. became the target of disgruntled citizens. Violence spread throughout the city, and the nation's leaders went into hiding, fearing the worst. The president's cabinet members and key Congressional leaders convened at a secret, top-security bunker in Virginia, where they would live for the foreseeable future.

Under this arrangement, the federal government continued to exist on a minimal level, but out of sight from the citizens. They were in contact with the top military generals, but America faced a serious problem—most of the nation's armed forces were overseas fighting other people's battles. Very few troops were available on U.S. soil to help quell the violence—or heaven forbid, to defend the country against an attack from a foreign power. America was at a boiling point, and the pot was about to boil over.

Within a week it became clear to the leaders of the Coalition that the United States government had fallen into disarray. The time had come to implement the second phase of their plan.

The Coalition could have easily launched dozens of nuclear weapons at the United States and annihilated the nation. But that would have worked against their goal of occupying the land, so a more traditional attack was needed. Their goal remained simple— eliminate all of America's current inhabitants and repopulate the cities and farms with their own countrymen.

So in accordance with the Coalition's plan, more than 300 Russian and Chinese warships soon departed their home ports and headed into international waters. The United States demanded an explanation, but they were told the ships were only performing "military exercises." These ships maneuvered through the oceans until they were positioned just a few hundred miles from each of America's largest coastal cities. The United States continued to protest these "exercises," but the nation's inner turmoil soon overshadowed the quiet movements of the Coalition forces.

Each ship carried several armored tanks loaded on transport trucks and thousands of battle-ready soldiers. The ships were also equipped with hundreds of powerful missiles that would be launched if needed. But for now the Coalition leaders patiently waited to begin the attack, watching the oil embargo effectively tear America apart.

The Coalition soldiers certainly didn't mind waiting for the attack to begin, because it meant less of a chance they would be killed during the invasion. The Coalition had promised each soldier a large American home of their own once the attack was complete, so they good-naturedly spent their time debating whether they would rather have a mansion near the beach, a 1,000-acre cattle ranch, or a fancy cabin nestled away in the mountains. They could hardly believe their good fortune.

By mid-October, the American Dream was completely gone. For years, American citizens had been lulled into a sense of security that their government would always protect them and at least provide them with food stamps if times got tough, but now they could hardly find a piece of bread to eat. A large house filled with expensive furniture and two cars in the garage now meant absolutely nothing.

As the nation's collective hunger mounted, people began to act in ways they would have never imagined. There were reports of families killing each other over the contents of a refrigerator, and of mothers even killing their own children so they could have any remaining food for themselves.

Neighbors either fought each other or banded together and attacked other neighborhoods. This mob mentality led to levels of bloodshed that hadn't been seen on American soil since the Civil War.

In the midst of this turmoil, the Coalition ships were still being tracked by America's defense systems, and the U.S. president was fully aware of their movements. He met daily with the nation's military leaders, but they couldn't reach an agreement on how to respond to the Coalition's actions. The "military exercises" had been reported in the media, but the military hadn't revealed how dangerously close the Coalition ships actually were, fearing it would cause hysteria among the people.

After another lengthy meeting, the president finally made a decision. "We will do nothing at this time," he said. "It just doesn't make sense to attack them. Let them be the aggressors. How do we know they aren't just bluffing?"

The cabinet members shook his head. "This isn't a bluff. They are checking us for weaknesses. I think we need to attack some of their ships to send a message that we aren't intimidated."

"No," the president responded. "If we strike first, we would likely start a nuclear war that would forever change our way of life. If we are going to war, they need to make the first move."

Several of the military advisors grumbled. "You really aren't going to do anything?" one man shouted. "Isn't that simply a cowardly way to admit defeat?"

The president shook his head. "Don't you see we are in a precarious situation? One bad choice could erase our country from the face of the earth. Most of our troops are overseas. Our only real option is to play dead. Let the enemy think the government is destroyed. It will probably cause their attack to be less severe than it otherwise would be. It is our best hope to survive and rise again."

Very few leaders agreed with the president, but he was now acting as the Commander in Chief, and he made that clear by making sure his bodyguards controlled the bunker's communications equipment. A person would have to leave the safety of the bunker to alert the nation, but no one was willing to do so.

The president's decision had a direct effect on the nation's military. Most American soldiers on active duty in the United States would have gladly gone to battle if they had been notified an enemy attack was imminent, but all forms of communication from their commanders had ceased. After staying at their posts for several days without any assurance they would be paid or even fed, nearly all of them had finally departed to find their loved ones.

The Coalition leaders received continual reports of what was happening in America's cities from their spy satellites. They welcomed each new report with delight, laughing at what they called "the American crybabies." They could never have predicted the overwhelming chaos that had overtaken American society. They had expected at least some kind of military opposition, but it looked like it was going to be a cakewalk to occupy the country.

"We should have done this years ago," the Coalition leaders told each other.

Even though the Coalition was completely confident of victory and they wanted to keep the cities intact, they finally decided to fire a few conventional missiles into major cities and then unleash the soldiers from the ships along both coasts. It would terrify the American citizens and send them scurrying inland like mice, where they could be rounded up and exterminated.

The ships began launching missiles just before dawn the next morning, aiming at a few prominent landmarks in Los Angeles and New York City. Several of those cities' tallest skyscrapers were toppled within minutes, showering enormous amounts of rubble onto the streets. Missiles were then fired into a few other cities, and the attacks accomplished the goal of scattering the people.

Later that day the Coalition ships docked at several ports. Thousands of Coalition soldiers rushed into the cities, all dressed in their distinctive light-colored uniforms and armed with high-powered rifles and small swords. As the soldiers moved inland, they showed no mercy, using their swords to viciously cut down any American they came across, no matter whether it was a man, woman or child. The soldiers had been told to save their ammunition for later, in case they met any real resistance.

As news of the Coalition's invasion came across President Johnson's laptop, the Jolley's Ranch members were stunned.

"We should stop for the day," President Johnson said. "I don't think any of us feels like doing anything but mourning the loss of our fellow citizens."

They were near the Red Rocks picnic area in Diamond Fork Canyon, and so they set up camp there. Once they were settled, President Johnson put the laptop on a handcart and turned up the volume so everyone could hear the Church's reports from around the nation on what was happening.

"Are you sure this is for real?" a man asked.

"Of course it is," Doug said, feeling a little angry. "What do you think we've been preparing for during the past several months? This is it—the start of World War III, and our country is hardly prepared for it."

The faithful Church members in California had gathered at the smaller, more inland temples, and they were sending steady text messages to Church headquarters. The most pertinent messages were then read over the network by a reporter.

The California members said they had felt the Lord's protection, but they said the sky was black with smoke from the damaged coastal cities. They also reported that in the past couple of hours, thousands of people had been seen fleeing on foot along the freeways heading toward the mountains. Curiously, no one stopped at the temples. They just kept running, hoping to stay ahead of the enemy soldiers that were now moving inland.

The strangest report coming from each city was that convoys of 18-wheeled Coalition trucks were ignoring the large cities and were immediately getting on the major freeways heading inland. These trucks each carried two armored tanks. One report said a large truck convoy was moving along I-80 through California and heading into Nevada.

"What could that mean?" Becky asked Doug. "Why would they worry about transporting tanks here? You'd think they would just bomb us."

Doug felt weak. "They are probably more worried about conquering the people, rather than destroy the cities. Tanks can easily accomplish the task of subduing the citizens, and I'm sure the Wasatch Front is a prime target. We need to get to Manti as soon as possible."

As the day wore on, the Coalition convoy steadily traveled east on I-80, only stopping to receive fuel from their accompanying refueling trucks. They had also done their homework, knowing where every fuel repository was along the way. This allowed them to refill the trucks every couple of hours.

Doug was right about where the tanks were being transported, but he didn't realize their true target. The tanks' mission was to reach key U.S. military installations and occupy them. The Coalition expected some opposition at each military base from any remaining military personnel, but the tanks should easily quash any opposition.

When those bases were under Coalition control, it would simply be a matter of getting rid of the remaining U.S. citizens before the Coalition countries could occupy the land.

CHAPTER 24

Once the Jolley's Ranch group heard about the Coalition tanks that were headed toward Utah, all thoughts of resting disappeared. They quickly packed up their camp and continued their journey down Diamond Fork Canyon. Their group sent scouts ahead to survey the road, and they reported that the highway pass through Billy's Mountain above the Thistle Landslide was now nothing but piles of rocks.

The mountain had come down on both sides, burying the road and making the road completely impassable. They considered climbing over the rocks, but there were more boulders perched above the road and ready to tumble down at any moment. It wasn't worth risking the lives of the camp members.

"The only other option is to cross the landslide itself," President Johnson said. Doug agreed, but it would be a definite challenge.

The following afternoon the group found themselves at the base of the landslide, trying to determine how to cross it. When the slide had first blocked the canyon in 1983, it had been nearly 120 feet high. But after the recent earthquakes and the soaking from the recent hailstorm, another large portion of the mountain had come down, turning the slide into a 250-foot-high barrier of unstable soil.

"I don't know how we are going to get over it without abandoning our handcarts," President Johnson said as they stared upward at the slide. "And there's really no way around it. The mud has even closed off the railroad tunnels, so that's out of the question, too."

At that moment a report came across the Church's network

that the Coalition convoy traveling on I-80 had reached Utah and the tanks had been unloaded at the Tooele Army Depot west of Salt Lake City. The tanks had destroyed the buildings there, and the attack had unleashed a white cloud of ash that was drifting toward the Wasatch Front. The report concluded by saying, "This cloud is potentially toxic. All camps in the Wasatch mountains immediately take shelter in your tents and stay inside until further notice!"

Doug and the other leaders leapt into action. Their tents were still piled on the wagon, but they spread them out along the old highway and assembled them in a line on the roadway. They had most of them set up within five minutes, just as the sky above them turned from bright blue to yellowish white.

"Get in the tents and close every opening," President Johnson yelled. "Don't come out until we say so. This ash could kill you."

As the last tent door was zipped up, white ash drifted down from the sky and covered their tents. Most of the tents had small plastic windows, and the camp members looked in astonishment at the strange dust that was settling on the camp. It looked harmless, like a light snow, but reports began to come in from the Salt Lake Valley that citizens who hadn't taken shelter were showing strange symptoms, such as seizures.

The danger apparently came from breathing the ash, rather than having it touch your skin. Doug suspected that the cloud contained hazardous particles from the chemical weapons that had been stored at the Tooele depot for many years.

Doug was particularly worried about Becky and the unborn child she was carrying. She always went the extra mile and had been one of the last people setting up tents, long after the other women had gone inside. He berated himself for not making her go into the tent sooner. He prayed that her act of service wouldn't come back to haunt them.

Everyone stayed inside their tents throughout the day. The children were crying, because in everyone's haste to get in the tents, most of the food supplies had been left on the wagons.

✤ ✤ ✤

President Johnson had asked Doug to join him in his tent, and they listened intently to the messages coming from the Church. The Coalition convoy had entered the Salt Lake Valley after leaving Tooele, but then had turned north on I-15 and traveled to Hill Air Force Base, where a few stalwart, patriotic Air Force personnel were waiting for them. Two F-16 fighter jets were soon in the air, and within minutes six tanks were destroyed. But soon the remaining four tanks had somehow shot down both planes. The tanks then destroyed the base's runways, making them unusable. Finally, the tanks rampaged through the base, destroying buildings and crushing vehicles.

One of the tanks fired into a weapons supply warehouse, sparking an enormous explosion that resembled a miniature atomic bomb. It shook the entire region and the plume of smoke went several miles into the sky.

With their work completed, the tanks headed south again. They sped through the Salt Lake Valley, crossed the Point of the Mountain and were soon in Utah County.

"It's clear they are going to military bases," President Johnson said. "What do you think is their next target?"

"Probably the military bases around Denver and Colorado Springs," Doug said. "If they are following a map, they might try to take a shortcut to I-70 by taking Highway 6 through Spanish Fork Canyon—and we'll be right in their path."

A steady rain began to fall, adding to the camp's misery. Then came the report they had dreaded.

"Here is an update for all Saints in the camps along the Wasatch Front. The convoy carrying enemy tanks has passed Springville and exited I-15 at Spanish Fork. They are on Highway 6 and appear to be heading to Spanish Fork Canyon. Any camps in Spanish Fork Canyon are in severe danger! You must hide immediately!"

Doug was stunned. They could stay in the tents and get crushed by the tanks, or leave them and be exposed to the lingering ash from Tooele. Maybe the rain would lessen the ash's effects. He and President Johnson said a quick prayer.

"What answer did you receive?" Doug asked.

President Johnson said, "The Spirit is shouting, 'Get the heck out of here!'"

A few miles to the north, Tad and Emma had finally felt well enough to leave the Springville Evergreen Cemetery and begin traveling again toward Spanish Fork Canyon. Tad's foot was feeling much better after the day's rest. Then they saw the white cloud develop in the western sky and knew it wasn't natural.

"We need to get to the cemetery office," Tad said. They went across the road and the door was broken open, but the office was in pretty good shape.

Tad started going through a cupboard. "The cemetery workers probably used some sort of mask when they sprayed chemicals to kill weeds and insects. Look for something like that."

Emma opened a drawer and found two gas masks. "Good job," Tad said. "I think you just saved our lives."

The ash began to fall, and they discussed staying in the office another day, but both of them had a sense of urgency to get to Manti. So they put the masks on and started walking. The masks were hard to breathe through, but it was better than the alternative.

They walked through Mapleton toward the canyon, and late in the day they reached Highway 6 near the mouth of Spanish Fork Canyon. Just then the ground seemed to shake. "Is it another earthquake?" Emma asked.

Tad didn't answer. Instead, Tad looked past her, then pulled her off the side of the road into some bushes. Within seconds, large trucks carrying four tanks rumbled past them, followed by a fuel truck. Tad stammered, "Those aren't American tanks. What is going on?"

Emma was shocked by this new development. "Maybe they were the cause of the cloud we saw," she said.

Tad was just as disturbed. "We might not want to go into the canyon yet," he said. "Let's stay here and pray for our children."

At the foot of the Thistle Landslide, the priesthood leaders urged the Saints to come out of their tents. President Johnson quickly explained the situation. "We need to leave everything and climb over the slide. Otherwise the tanks are going to kill us."

Two men went ahead of the group and created a small trail. Then the women and children began the climb. The men followed them, carrying a child if needed. It was still lightly raining, and everyone struggled with each step on the muddy slope, but ten minutes later they had all miraculously made it to the top of the landslide.

As the rest of the group hurried down the other side, Doug and President Johnson stayed hidden near the top, waiting to see if the convoy would arrive. Within five minutes they appeared. They stayed on Highway 6, but soon came to Billy's Mountain and saw that the highway was now covered by boulders.

The trucks were too long to turn around, and the tanks were unloaded to see if they could make it through the pass. But it quickly became apparent that it was too dangerous.

A few of the Coalition soldiers looked down into the canyon. Doug could see them pointing at the group's tents.

"Great, they've seen our tents," he said.

Within minutes the tanks were rumbled back down the highway and took the small road into the Spanish Fork River Campground, the same route taken by the Jolley's Ranch group. The tanks stopped briefly as they came upon the campsite, but then like bloodthirsty animals the tank drivers mercilessly ran over the tents and smashed the handcarts.

Finally one of the tanks stopped, and three uniformed soldiers got out. They lifted up the tents and seemed disappointed to not find any human victims inside. One of the soldiers pointed to the slide, and even with the rain it was evident where the group had climbed up just a few minutes before. They soldiers returned to their tank and it drove over to the base of the slide.

Doug turned to President Johnson. "We didn't exactly cover our tracks too well, did we?"

The tank slowly inched its way upward, following the trail the Saints had made. The tank was making amazing progress, climbing nearly 50 feet up the slope.

President Johnson turned to the group below him and shouted, "A tank is climbing up the slide! Pray like you never have before! Ask the Lord for protection!"

Instantly the Saints united in prayer, calling upon the Lord. The tank moved forward another few feet, but it was no match for the group of pleading Saints on the other side of the slide.

Within a minute, the heavens opened. The rain started coming down so hard that Doug could barely see the tank, but he saw it slip a little. Then the slide shifted under the tank's weight. The tank spun its tracks furiously, but it only succeeded in partially burying itself. The rain seemed to get even stronger, and finally the tank reversed its course and backed down to the canyon floor.

Another tank gave it a try, but it hardly got 15 feet up the slope before sliding down. After about a minute, the tanks changed course and headed back to the main road where the transport trucks had finally turned around. The tanks were quickly loaded onto the trucks and whisked back down the canyon.

"The tanks are gone!" Doug called out to the group.

The Saints gave a shout of thanksgiving. They were covered in mud, soaked to the bone, and their belongings had been smashed, but they were grateful to a merciful Heavenly Father who had spared their lives.

The rain stopped within a few minutes, and the Saints crossed back over the slide to inspect their belongings. Most of the tent poles were snapped, and many of the handcarts were beyond repair. But there were enough salvageable food and handcarts that they would be able to make it to Manti without too many hunger pains. They wouldn't have much shelter the rest of the way, but it was a great feeling to know they would be in Manti soon.

As the group started down the road, Doug stood on the top of the slide and looked back down the canyon. Where was Emma?

"Brother Dalton, let's go," President Johnson said. "It's more important that we get the group safely to Manti. Then you can come back to look for your sister."

Doug reluctantly nodded and joined the group.

At the mouth of the canyon, Tad and Emma waited nervously in the bushes alongside the road for nearly an hour. They didn't want to be caught in the canyon if the tanks returned.

Then they heard a familiar rumbling as the convoy of tanks appeared again. "The canyon must be blocked somehow!" Emma said. "Maybe they didn't see our group."

Once the tanks had passed them and were out of sight, Tad and Emma hurried up the side of the hill to see where they had gone—and to make sure they weren't coming back. The tanks were soon out of sight.

"I think we're safe for now," Emma said. "Let's see if we can catch up with the others."

The Church network later reported the Coalition convoy had returned to I-15 and traveled south, connecting with I-70 near Cove Fort, and were soon destroying military bases in Colorado.

CHAPTER 25

By nightfall the Jolley's Ranch group had made it a few miles closer to Manti, finally arriving at the little white LDS church along the highway in the town of Birdseye. They were greeted by two men who were acting as guards there. Once the men realized they were a group of Saints, they opened the church and let the group have some decent accommodations for the first time in a while. Most of the women and children were able to fit into the meetinghouse, while the men slept outside in the parking lot.

One of the building's guards introduced himself to Doug. "I'm Richard Dalton. I heard one of the men call you Brother Dalton, so I couldn't help but wonder if we are related."

Doug looked at Richard's blond hair and mustache and it was as if he was looking at one of his uncles. "Just by looking at you, I would almost guarantee it," he said. "Those Dalton genes shine right through, don't they?"

They talked for a few minutes and realized they were cousins through Finity Dalton who had settled in Wasatch County more than a century earlier.

"Well, it is a certainly a pleasure to meet you," Richard said. "Is there any way I can help you out?"

Doug nodded. "Actually there is. My sister and her husband are somewhere in this canyon, probably down past the Thistle slide. We have their kids with us, but I'm really worried about them."

Richard pondered for a moment. "Well, I've got a pair of horses at a barn not far from here. Why don't you and I go for a ride first thing in the morning to see if we can find them?"

"You'd really do that?" Doug asked.

Richard smiled. "You bet, especially for family."

The next morning as the camp prepared to depart, Doug told President Johnson of Richard's offer, and he was happy to hear about it. "That will be wonderful," the president said. "Just catch up to us when you can."

Ten minutes later the two men were swiftly riding down the road toward the Thistle slide. After a few miles, Doug noticed two figures scamper into the bushes about 100 yards ahead of them. He motioned for Richard to stop. "I saw some people running in front of us," he said.

They approached the area where Doug had seen the people, and he called out, "Emma! Tad! Is that you?"

"Doug! Over here!" a man shouted.

Doug whirled around and could see Tad and Emma huddled on the hill under a bush. "Woo-hoo! You're safe!"

The couple hurried down the hill, and Doug hopped off his horse to give his sister a big hug. Then he even gave Tad a hug. "I'm so glad to see you both alive," he said. "Did you see the tanks?"

"We sure did," Tad said. "We found the remains of your tents, and handcarts, and it looked pretty scary. But there weren't any bodies, so that was a good sign. We've been praying that our kids are safe."

"Yes, they are fine. The whole camp has been blessed and protected by the Lord," Doug said. He then introduced them to Richard, and they started back toward the main group. Emma rode behind Richard, which allowed Doug and Tad to patch up their differences as they galloped along. Within minutes they were friends again.

The group had traveled about a mile by the time the horses caught up to them. Doug looked for the North children, and stopped the horse near them. He called out, "Are there any kids here who want to see their parents?"

Tad hopped off the horse and ran to the children as Richard helped Emma down from his horse. David, Charles, and Leah could hardly believe that their father had returned. The children and parents all joined in a group hug, and then the rest of the group was introduced to Tad. After the despair he had felt, he now felt truly happy and surrounded by unconditional love.

Doug climbed down from his horse, handed the reins to Richard, then gave him a warm handshake. "Thank you for your help," Doug told him. "This means so much to us."

Richard smiled. "No problem. Have a good trip to Manti. You should be there within a few days, but you know where to find me if you need me!"

Tad asked Doug to examine his injured foot. The swelling had gone down, but the pain had increased. Doug gently checked it and found two broken bones and some muscle damage.

"You shouldn't have walked on this," Doug said. "We need to get it immobilized so it can heal."

Tad playfully clasped his brother-in-law on the shoulder and laughed. "I wish somebody had told me that two weeks ago before I walked all over the valley! I might as well just keep walking."

But despite his protests, Tad was soon reclining comfortably in one of the handcarts, with David and Charles happily pulling their dad up the road. They told him all about their adventures at the Jolley's Ranch camp, and Tad loved hearing his sons' stories.

Throughout that day the group kept a steady pace on the paved highway and climbed into the Sanpete Valley, reaching the town of Fairview by nightfall. They were greeted there by several Saints who directed them to gather at the town's red-brick church on the main road. The Jolley's Ranch members found it interesting that these members were still living in their own houses.

Doug asked one of the men, "Haven't you been told to gather to Manti?"

"We have, and most of the town has done so. But those of us who are still here have the special assignment to help and encourage each group as it arrives here," the man said. "We give everyone a good turkey dinner to give you a boost of strength as you get ready to walk the last few miles to Manti. They told us about 20 groups would be passing through, but you're the first one we've seen!"

Doug was happy to hear other groups were also gathering to Manti. It hadn't been officially announced, but he sensed that the Saints gathering to this valley would someday leave as a group for Missouri and then lay the foundation of New Jerusalem.

Since joining the group earlier that day, Tad had felt some unspoken animosity toward him from some of the Saints. They knew his past, and wondered if he could be trusted. So that night he asked President Johnson if he could take a few minutes to tell the group what he had experienced. He told them about the hailstorm, the earthquake and the flood, and then he answered some questions about how he had escaped from Officer Fernelius and had cut the chip out of his hand by himself. He had the group hanging on his every word.

As the night came to a close, Tad made it clear that he wasn't proud of what he had done over the past few months. "You are the true heroes," he told the group. "I admire every one of you. When I was all alone on West Mountain, I finally realized what was truly important—my family. I will never forget it. The Lord gave me a second chance, and I am going to make the most of it."

Tad's words seemed to soften the hearts of those who had doubted his sincerity, and afterward he received several welcoming handshakes from those same members.

Later that night as everyone was settling into their sleeping bags, Tad took Bishop Cluff aside and gave him the backpack he had been wearing. "Bishop, please guard this pack carefully. Inside you will find my tithing for the past several months. I know with all of the economic troubles going on in the nation, it might be mostly a symbolic payment, rather than one that could be used to purchase anything, but I feel I need to honorably pay it."

Bishop Cluff opened the backpack and saw the plastic bags

filled with money. "Thank you, Brother North, although I'm afraid I don't have a receipt for you! But as soon as we get to Manti I'll make sure it is given to the proper priesthood leaders."

Tad shook the bishop's hand gratefully, and for the first time in several months, he felt worthy to hold the priesthood. It was a feeling he had missed and never wanted to live without again.

Two days later, the group passed through the city of Ephraim and could soon see the Manti Temple in the distance, beckoning to them. As they got within a mile of the temple, they could see what appeared to be a shimmering white sea in the fields surrounding the temple hill. But the group soon realized it was actually hundreds of white tents set up in preparation for the arrival of the mountain camps.

As the group moved closer to the temple, a Church leader met them and welcomed them to "Camp Manti." He led them to a cluster of tents in a field directly north of the temple, and they quickly settled in. Over the next few days, the Jolley's Ranch members were put to work helping gather a large harvest of fruits and vegetables. The Lord had certainly blessed the valley that summer. The area's numerous turkey and cattle farms were also thriving, and there was plenty of meat for everyone.

In some ways, life at the Manti camp felt a bit like paradise. The group knew other trials likely awaited them, but they savored this brief time of peace.

One evening a few days after their arrival in Manti, Emma asked Leah to go for a walk with her. They stayed on a dirt road for a while, but eventually they left the road and walked through a nearby field toward the setting sun.

The two shared a special bond, and Emma had received several premonitions about her young daughter. She had never shared these feelings yet with Leah, but she knew that the beautiful blonde child walking next to her would yet play a great role in the Lord's kingdom.

As Emma quietly pondered her daughter's future, a curious bank of clouds had covered the mountains. As the sun shone through the clouds, it seemed almost like heaven itself was descending on the valley.

Emma stopped to watch the clouds, but Leah walked several yards ahead of her into a waist-high field of wild grass. It appeared she was being drawn to the light.

Leah was wearing a white dress, and Emma could easily envision her daughter someday watching the Savior's millennial arrival in a similar way.

Leah finally turned back to her mother and said, "Aren't the clouds beautiful? I could look at them forever."

CHAPTER 26

The first weekend of October had come and gone without a General Conference. With all of the commotion in the world, the First Presidency had announced General Conference would be held sometime later in the year.

Finally the official word came that there would be one session of General Conference. It would be broadcast on the Church network on the final Sunday of October at 10 a.m.

The Saints in Manti were invited to gather on the lawn of the Manti Temple to listen to the conference. The large speakers that had been used for many years as part of the Mormon Miracle Pageant were in place, and hymns were being broadcast as the Saints gathered.

It had turned out to be a chilly morning, but everyone was in good spirits. So much had taken place since the April Conference that it seemed like years since the Church members had heard a live broadcast from the prophet himself.

At 9:50 a.m., several men removed a large tarp from a platform at the base of the temple. No one had paid any attention to it until now.

"What is it?" Emma asked.

"It looks like a pulpit and a television camera," Doug said. There was also a large screen behind the pulpit.

Within moments two men in dark suits emerged and stood near the pulpit. One of the men leaned over to the microphone and said, "Please stand. We are privileged to have with us today our beloved prophet."

A unified gasp rose from the crowd, and everyone stood as a man moved toward the pulpit. Everyone recognized the well-known walk of the President of the Church. He was getting older, but still had a spring in his step. The television camera switched on, and the prophet's image was broadcast on the large screen. He waved to the crowd, and many people were openly weeping.

"The prophet is here?" Leah asked.

"Yes, that's him," Emma said, shedding tears of joy.

The prophet stepped to the podium. "Good morning, my dear brothers and sisters. You seem a bit surprised to see me!"

The crowd laughed, and he continued, "I am grateful to the good brethren who helped me arrive here yesterday from Salt Lake. We had a couple of close calls, but the Lord protected us, and I am honored to be among you."

He then explained that their meeting would serve as the General Conference of the Church, and his message would be broadcast to gatherings of the Saints across the world.

The prophet stepped aside briefly as the president of the Manti Temple gave an opening prayer, and then the prophet spoke to them again.

"Today I speak to you at the base of the majestic Manti Temple, built by faithful Latter-day Saints more than a century ago," he told the worldwide audience. "Those early Saints faced struggles of their own, but they overcame them and left this remarkable building as their legacy.

"At this time, it is our opportunity to create our own legacy on a much larger scale. We are the privileged generation that will build Zion, even the New Jerusalem. Each of you who are listening to my voice have been put through many trials over the past few months, yet you have stayed faithful. In order to create a Zion people, the Lord has put us through a sifting process. We all have friends, and even your own family members, who were considered active members of the Church just a year ago, but who are no longer a part of us. For whatever reason, they have chosen a different path.

"These trials haven't been easy, but they have prepared us for what lies ahead. I assure you that the troubles are far from over, but I also assure you that the Savior Jesus Christ is carefully watching over the members of this Church.

"We are now in the midst of a worldwide crisis that has long been prophesied. Do not despair. The very fact you are members of this Church at this crucial time in history shows that in the premortal world you were valiant children of our Heavenly Father. Now you are on the earth to help prepare the way for the Second Coming of our Lord."

The prophet cleared his throat, and then took on a glow as if heaven itself was shining down on him.

"The Church is in excellent shape and is functioning at full capacity. In these dangerous times, each of the apostles have spread out to serve in various ways throughout the world. We are like those first apostles of this dispensation called by Joseph Smith. We may be separated by distance, but we are united in purpose. By spreading out, we are assured that the proper priesthood keys will always be on the earth. The death of one of us will not cause the loss of these keys, since members of the First Presidency and the Quorum of the Twelve all hold the keys of this dispensation.

"If a member of the Quorum of the Twelve dies, another worthy man will be ordained to the quorum. In fact, the day will soon come when the Quorum of the Twelve will reunite in New Jerusalem. That will be a joyous day. But until that time, we will serve throughout the world proclaiming this gospel."

The prophet concluded by bearing his testimony of the truthfulness of the gospel and the latter-day work that was taking place. He promised the Saints that their current distress would only be for a short time. Then Zion's banner would be unfurled, beginning in New Jerusalem, for all the world to see.

Emma listened intently to every word, and her heart burned with a knowledge that the Lord would be watching over the Saints no matter what awaited them.

Following the meeting, the Norths and Daltons stood in line for more than an hour to shake hands with the prophet. When their turns came, he treated them kindly and asked each of the children their names. He told them how grateful he was that they had chosen to gather with the Saints.

"We just wanted to follow you," Charles said. "You're the prophet, you know."

The prophet smiled. "Thank you for saying that, but I want to remind you who is really in charge—the Lord Jesus Christ. I am only His mouthpiece. But I promise you that He is concerned about each one of you, and He wants you to stay faithful so you can build His kingdom. Can you all promise to stay faithful?"

The two families nodded in unison, and Emma heard Tad say under his breath, "I will." Tears came to her eyes, and she squeezed her husband's hand tightly.

The prophet left the valley in the late afternoon in an ordinary covered wagon led by horses. The Saints lined the roadway, and he waved to them as he passed by.

He had met briefly with the stake presidents before his departure, and among the things he told them was he would be staying in a protected mountain location for the next few months, and he would be in regular contact with them through the Church's satellite network.

A holy aura seemed to fill the Manti camp throughout the remainder of the day. The Saints felt recharged and ready to face whatever may await them.

Thousands of miles to the south, the Saints in Guatemala were gathered again on the hill behind the temple, and they rejoiced as they heard the prophet's words. The comments about New Jerusalem touched their hearts. Josh had already informed them of their upcoming journey, but hearing it from the prophet himself solidified it in their minds.

That night Josh and Mathoni met briefly outside the bus. No one had suspected the precious cargo of ancient plates that it held. They discussed the group's preparation, and they agreed everything was in order for the journey to Missouri. All they needed was the word from the First Presidency on when to begin moving north.

Josh smiled to himself as he looked at Mathoni. After living through so many centuries of darkness and turmoil, this special witness of the Savior was finally seeing the fruition of his efforts.

"Your excitement is contagious," Josh told him. "You're like a kid on Christmas morning."

Mathoni laughed. "You don't know how true that is. Now the fun is really going to begin. During some of those slow times over the past 20 centuries I often thought of the earth's final days, and now they are here!"

Josh had wanted to ask Mathoni some specific questions about the future, and he thought this might be a good time. "On our bus ride, you had mentioned that I might play a role in the Lord's kingdom. What do I need to do to prepare myself?"

"You are on the right path, and you don't need to know anything else, besides just doing your best every day. Then you'll find yourself in the right place at the right time. I really can't say more."

"I know," Josh said. "I'm just glad to have met you and to be able to learn from your example."

"Thank you, that means a lot," Mathoni said. "I guess why I don't want to say much about the future is because the next few years are going to be so exciting I can't properly describe them. It will feel like one big extravaganza after another. There will always be some obstacles, and that is to be expected, but I promise you this—we are going to have a blast!"

THE NEXT STEP

―――――― ❧ ――――――

The past twelve months had been filled with temporal upheaval and spiritual growth for the Norths, the Daltons, and the Browns. Would anything in the future exceed what they had just experienced?

Most definitely.

In the days following the prophet's visit to Manti, the families prepared for winter. There would be little time for rest, however. As spring approached, they would participate in events that would transform the world.

Doug had no idea he would soon meet with an apostle and be called to scour the earth one last time looking for people who are seeking the truth.

Nor did Tad know he would be a leader in a military group of LDS men who called themselves "The Elders of Israel" that would step forth from the Rocky Mountains to battle the Coalition forces.

And Josh and Kim could never have anticipated the unique experiences their group would face—even with one of the Three Nephites helping them—during their journey from Guatemala to Missouri.

Finally, with their husbands away, Emma and Becky's lives would take surprising turns as they prepare their families to travel to Missouri and help build the greatest city of all—New Jerusalem.

Read about these exciting events as the *Standing in Holy Places* series continues in *Book Two: The Celestial City*.

ABOUT THE AUTHOR

———— ✦ ————

Chad Daybell has written more than 20 books for the LDS market. He is known for his bestselling novels such as *Chasing Paradise* and *The Emma Trilogy*, as well as his non-fiction books for youth, including *The Aaronic Priesthood* and *The Youth of Zion*. He and his wife Tammy also created the *Tiny Talks* series for Primary children.

Chad has worked in the publishing business for the past two decades. He is currently the president of Spring Creek Book Company, one of the leading LDS publishing firms.

Visit **www.springcreekbooks.com** to see the company's lineup of popular titles.

Learn about Chad and the upcoming volumes in the *Standing in Holy Places* series at his personal website **www.cdaybell.com**.